John Boorman looking across the years at Sebastian Rice Edwards, who plays him as a young boy in *Hope and Glory*.

Hope and Glory

by the same author

MONEY INTO LIGHT
The Emerald Forest: A Diary

Hope and Glory

John Boorman

faber and faber

LONDON · BOSTON

First published in 1987
by Faber and Faber Limited
3 Queen Square London WC1N 3AU

Photoset and printed in Great Britain by
Redwood Burn Limited, Trowbridge, Wiltshire

British Library Cataloguing in Publication Data

Boorman, John, *1933*–
Hope and glory.
I. Title
822'.914   PR6052.O57/

ISBN 0–571–14983–9

Contents

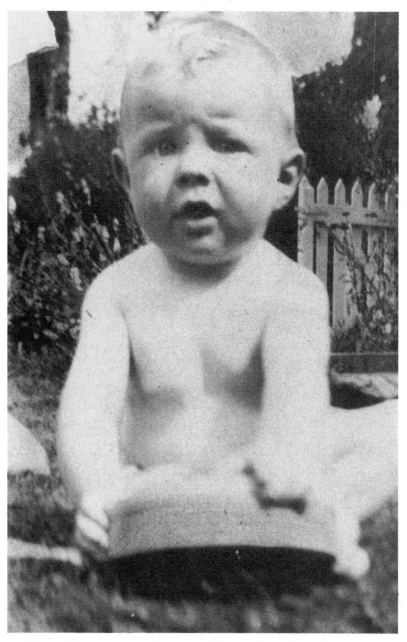

Me, aged six months, outside my grandfather's bungalow at Shepperton.
I am facing the river, sitting in a chocolate box.

A Memoir

The script that follows was once a precious document, studied by technicians, pored over by art directors, memorized by actors, analysed, budgeted, scheduled by accountants and production managers, synopsized by studio script departments, and clung to by me like a life raft during stormy moments of the shoot.

Now it is a relic, a husk, purpose served, vitality spent. The movie has outgrown it, outstripped it, bettered it, left home. The scenes I changed, edited-out or truncated in post-production remain in this fourth draft screenplay and irritate me no end. Nevertheless, I have left it as it was just before shooting began since it represents my intentions at that point. The fourth draft was a staging post, taking the place of earlier drafts, and being superseded in turn by the film. I had made previous attempts at the subject going back some fifteen years, which for good and bad reasons were abandoned; of course, behind and beyond these forays was life itself, mine at least, a childhood and a family.

It occurred to me that it might be illuminating to chart, as it were, the history of an enterprise that began with stories told to my children at bedtime. They seldom wearied of my adventures as a child during the war: air-raids, barrage balloons, shrapnel, doodlebugs, crystal sets; then the move to the Thames at Shepperton and the wonders of the river, punts and kingfishers, a non-anthropomorphic *Wind in the Willows*.

When I gave my eldest daughter, Telsche, the first draft script to read she tossed it back after twenty minutes. 'You couldn't possibly have read it so soon,' I cried with all the pent-up paranoia of an author exposing his work for the first time. 'Well,' she said in qualification, 'I skipped all the stories I knew, which didn't leave much, did it?'

3

My first foray into the territory was for television. It was inspired by my admiration, affection and, indeed, awe for my mother and her three sisters. The plan was to film my own children asking them about their past, sitting at their feet and listening to their stories. The four sisters tend to talk all at once, and yet such is their harmony, they never appear to interrupt each other, the trick being that it is not, by any means, all talk: they make sounds, oohs and aahs, cooing and laughter, sighing and tutting. They gurgle and giggle. There are encouraging sounds, so-sorry sounds, amazement sounds, appreciative sounds. They orchestrate these noises around the melody line of the speaking sister of the moment. Their china-blue eyes are full of wonder: they remember, they remind each other, they bubble over. They were, and are, a beautiful quartet of women who still call themselves the 'Chapman Girls'. We define ourselves in the stories we tell and by the stories we remember, and as they would be telling their stories, from time to time, I intended to 'flashback' and evoke their childhood days in dramatized scenes. *My* daughters would play *their* parts. When they told stories of me, my son Charley would act me as a boy. I would do the role of *their* father, *my* own grandfather. It would be incest as an art form.

It was to be an attempt to look at a family, up and down the generations, backwards and sideways, and this inverted role-playing would perhaps say something about the movement of blood and genes.

Finally I funked it. I could predict the problems all too clearly. It would be like trying to organize charades at Christmas, and I had a dread insight that the result might be similar.

Other films intervened, but my thoughts often returned to the subject, perhaps because when I wasn't making movies I spent much of my time helping my wife raise a family in a world where family life was disintegrating. In 1968 I had made two films in Hollywood, *Point Blank* and *Hell in the Pacific*. We had our six little green cards and a house on the beach in the Malibu Colony. Telsche and Katrine went to the local school and learned to recite the Oath of Allegiance with American accents. While California was bizarre, I could deal with it; when it started to seem normal, I panicked. I felt my grip on reality slipping; my neighbours became translucent before my eyes, they spoke in loud voices in an unknown tongue. For reassurance and human warmth we sought out the 'shadow' population, the Japanese gardeners, Mexican maids, black housekeepers, who came in in waves each morning to Malibu, Beverly Hills and Bel Air. We bought goat's milk from Hillbillies scratching a living on a couple of acres of scrub in the Malibu mountains. These touchstones notwithstanding, our girls were soon sun-soaked, marinated in Coca Cola and blanding by the day. We fled to Ireland, a leap into the past, a turning back of the clock: convents, creeping bogs, crackling telephones, flickering and fading lights, and people drenched in rain-melancholy, both doom-laden and light-hearted, always ready to take flight on their own words or to sink under their weight.

In an eighteenth-century child's drawing of a house, in a valley hidden by oak and beech and enfolded in hills, our children grew up, taking country potions instead of vitamins, living in a chrysalis of old tales, superstitions and folk memory. Convalescent from LA future shock, we fell back together into myth.

I was once again, as I had been as a child, living out a family life that shut out much of the world, that turned in on itself. Not a nuclear family, but a solar system, all the bodies turning in harmonious orbit, the tensions equal and opposite; all were free to move but none could escape or break away without shattering the house, the valley, the family and sending the fragments scattering into the present world beyond. *She* was at the centre, magnetic. Three daughters joined to the matrix, one son.

So I had found my way back, into a place of women, dancing to the steps of Isis, recreating the conditions of childhood.

I had two sisters and no brother, and besides the three aunts there was my father's sister. He had no brothers either. When my father went to war he left me with a house full of women, with no male to curb their female excesses: the inexplicable and sudden tears, then the crass conspiratorial laughter at some sexual allusion in shocking carelessness of their mystery, and

5

the bleeding, and the stifling embraces when a boy's face was pressed into that infinite softness, falling, falling, inhaling all those layers of odour only scantily concealed by lily of the valley: acute, knotted, scarlet-blushing, shameful embarrassment.

Something of that shame comes back in a nauseous wave when I oblige my hand to set down the following words: I was born at No. 50 Rosehill Avenue, Carshalton, a monotonous street of those semi-detached suburban houses of which *four million* were built between the wars. My father bought the house with a deposit of £50 and paid off the mortgage at 17 shillings and 6 pence per week. The purchase price was £676. I reconstructed Rosehill Avenue on a disused airfield at Wisley in Surrey for a cost of three-quarters of a million pounds. In point of fact, our 'Street' set looked much more like one we moved to in Ewell when I was two years old, such are the composites of movies and memory. Council estates were springing up around Rosehill Avenue, rehousing London's slum-dwellers. My parents, like other home-owning semi-dwellers, had only a murky view of their place in the class system, but an acute sense of gentility which was affronted by council houses. They saw with mounting horror that my older sister, Wendy, came home from school swearing and talking 'common'. At ten she had caught doses of working-class diseases like scabies, scarlet fever and incipient Socialism from these fugitive kids from Bermondsey. She and my father argued and rowed. He was not a snob, certainly never despised those below him, but he deeply respected his superiors, felt threatened if things and people were not properly in their places. He was a sentimental patriot, a passionate royalist, a dogged Tory. His views were thinly thought out, and when challenged by Wendy, he would go white with rage, tremble and shake and bark out inarticulate defences of his besieged positions. His anger would cause him to mangle his usually immaculate platitudes into glorious surreal *non sequiturs*: 'I will not stand by and listen to you insult the country I fought and died for.'

Father had to choke back barrack-room insults that he would dearly have loved to hurl at his daughter Wendy to refute her political heresies. Red in the face, words twisted and strangled in his throat, he would bowdlerize some savage slogan into monumental ineffectiveness.

'You don't know your . . . your . . .' (oh to find a euphemism, yet preserve the alliteration) '. . . your apron from your elbow.'

Even Wendy was stopped in her tracks by that one.

He insisted that whenever the National Anthem was played over the wireless we all stood rigidly to attention, chin in, chest out, shoulders back, fists clenched with thumbs pointing down the seams of the trousers. He once caught me lying in bed with the Anthem playing on my crystal set. 'On your feet,' he commanded. It was a cold wartime winter night and bedrooms were never heated.

I whimpered a rather inventive excuse: 'If I stood up, the lead on the earphones is not long enough, so I wouldn't hear it anyway.'

'You don't have to hear it, son,' he said in his paternal imparting-of-wisdom voice. 'As long as you *know* it's playing, somewhere, you stand up.'

'But, Dad, it's freezing.'

He weakened, his manner softened. 'Just this once, then. But *lie* to attention. Remember, thumbs pointing down the seams of your pyjamas.'

Wendy would argue that being a Tory was against his own interests, that he was sustaining the class that oppressed us. But voting Conservative was a way of reassuring himself that he was not slipping into the dreaded pit of the working class. The *Daily Express* gave essential comfort to his views each morning, which was just as well for me since I was possessed by Rupert Bear. Benign and soothing it may have been to others, but to me there was a sinister tension about it; each day I anticipated some fearful happening which, of course, never came. I don't know if this was evil bile seeping out of the editorial pages or, more likely, the resonances in the brilliant drawings. Freedom and adventure were perfectly expressed by Rupert's fat little airplane with an open cockpit. I could never admit it then, but I liked it even better than the Spitfire.

7

My shame at being born in Rosehill Avenue comes partly from the political attitudes of my father, partly from the contumely and disdain heaped on Metroland, the world of the semi. 'Come, friendly bombs and fall on Slough,' smote Betjeman.

Four million built between the wars! So twelve, sixteen million people lived in them? Where did they come from? Where have they gone? May like me have kept quiet about their origins. I grew up wishing I had been higher born; then in the sixties, that I could claim to be lower born. Of course, fifty years on, most of these houses are still cared for, cherished with double glazing and pampered with patios, unlike the Radiant Cities that came later, the new towns, the tower blocks that have crumbled into dismay. Le Corbusier's manic followers descended like shock troops bringing more destruction to England than Hitler. They left a bleak and sterile landscape in their wake, but they left suburbia untouched except by their abuse.

Was there ever such a stealthy social revolution as the rise of this semi suburbia? They all missed it (or got it wrong) – the academics, the politicians, the upper classes. While they worried about Socialism and Fascism, the cuckoo had laid its egg in their nest and Margaret Thatcher would hatch out of it.

In London the Underground system pushed out spokes from the oily and grimy hub and the semis clustered about each station or ribboned along the new bypasses. Where did it come from, this new class? Some had slipped down from the middle class; most were dragging themselves up from the working class. They came from all parts and stations, disowning their lowly past, anaesthetizing it, so that most of the children I knew had no interest in where they came from, no memory of family history. We viewed each other with suspicion, kept ourselves to ourselves. Privacy protected our uncertainty about how to behave. On the whole we were enjoying a new prosperity. There was a garage for the Morris 8 or the Austin 7, a narrow strip of high-fenced garden for the children to play in. The private, inward-looking world of the nuclear family was taking shape. These dormitories, ten minutes' walk from the Tube, with no roots and no past, were home to a new phenomenon, as yet unnamed, the Commuter.

With the bonds of traditional society severed, they found themselves in a comfortably snug void. Filling that emptiness was the wireless. It played all day, banishing the dread silence, but there was seldom a reference to the semi suburbs in those programmes. The broadcasts came from a distant land where people spoke in alien accents as remote as the world unspooled each week at the Regal or the Odeon in American movies or snobbish English ones. We never imagined ever meeting such people or sharing their experiences, which isolated us further still. We lacked the skill to reflect on what we had become. We could not fathom ourselves. We took on the daft, foolish looks of institutionalized people, never certain how to speak or walk or behave. Grief embarrassed us; we shrank from gaiety, turned our faces from any kind of public display of feeling.

How wonderful was the war. It gave common cause, equal rations, community endeavour, but most delightful of all a myth, nurtured by wireless, newspaper and cinema, that allowed the semi people to leap their garden gates, vault over their embarrassments into the arms of patriotism.

The war was still to come. As yet in these streets there were no places of work, no schools, no shops, no churches, no sport, no pubs. During the day the men and the young were syphoned out to business and to learn; the wives were left to clean and polish, listen to the wireless and dream. Down these deserted streets, trading on the dreams and loneliness, came men knocking on the doors selling sheet music, magazines, vacuum cleaners, carpets, the man from the Pru collecting the weekly insurance premiums, the hire-purchase payments on the furniture and on and on. My mother would dig anxiously into her purse and sniff, seeking both money and sympathy, one of the many things that filled me with shame and embarrassment. It was worse when she was sniffing out money to buy *me* something. I determined that I would free myself as soon as I could from her brave self-sacrifice, fill her purse with money so that she would never again have to scrimp and scratch.

On Sundays the car was ceremoniously wheeled out from the garage, washed and polished, and the parents, with their two little tots tucked in the back, would motor off to the seaside or to Box Hill or to the Zoo at Whipsnade. They were home-owners, consumers, on a great adventure journeying into a myth of their own making.

Architects were contemptuous of the semi, not least because they were totally uninvolved in its design and construction. Those tasks fell to 'spec' builders who surely expressed the deep unconscious fantasies of a people oppressed by the patronizing values of its betters.

The past was wholly annihilated. Everything must be new and newly made, preferably in chrome and bakelite. Oh, how they broke free of the weight of tradition! The sun rose in stained glass over the front door, its rays splayed out on the garden gate, even the settee was shaped into sunbeams. The 'spec' builder lured us with promises of fresh air and sunshine, flowers and lawns, a refuge from the sooty cities and smoky slums. Tudor gables, leaded panes, bow windows – eclectic fragments from pre-Industrial Revolution England, from Robin Hood, pantomime stories, Ann Hathaway's cottage. Sometimes the rising sun gave way to a proud stained-glass galleon in full sail bearing the cross of St George, stirring atavistic yearnings in these down-trodden factory workers of diluted yeoman blood.

We had a teapot that was a chromium globe reflecting the whole universe, or at least the whole of our semi. The china, the cutlery, the carpets and curtains – all new, all in novel shapes and patterns. Clocks, vases, electric fires, cookers, streamlined and gleaming, all machine-made, banishing the craftsman, untouched by human hand.

Fitness, health, hygiene were all the rage. Hitler and Mussolini were admired before the war for their initiatives improving fitness and encouraging sport. Health usurped religion in this churchless, but not Godless, world. We were convalescents from the Industrial Revolution and needed several generations of fresh air and proper food to recover. Oh, what the English inflicted on the English: misery, deprivation and bondage on a scale that quite matched that visited on their colonial vassals. Half the population was wrenched from the land and into city slums where its past, its ways fell out of mind. And now here were the survivors fleeing to those new suburban streets, fugitives from the shocks, not only of the Industrial Revolution, but also of the First World War and the Depression. Forget all that, don't look back, reach forward into the smiling new world of the semis and sunshine, lawns and indoor lavatories. If you got through the Great War, escaped the mines, the foundries, the mills, then take comfort in amnesia and embrace the new myth, Arcadia for all.

We wore collars and ties now, and bowler hats. This was a new army of clerks, pen-pushers, a legion that leapt up to serve the new 'service industries', and who, after but a few years, would be made extinct by the digital computer and the button-pushers.

It was a massive migration. This was a new land, and the England of old was gone for ever. Its passing went unremarked because of the deceptive way it kept up appearances: church-spired villages watered by tumbling streams, wood smoke rising from thatch, a place of honour for the dead, the country wisdom of old men purchased for the price of a pint. The English country villages became, in truth, little more than movie sets, museums with working models. They pleased the eye, beguiled the heart, and the sham fed the folk myth. It was perhaps these faint echoes, like the impaired instincts of domestic animals, that sent us groping our way into those monotonous streets of semis, lured by a handful of cunning design metaphors that evoked an English past, yet paradoxically broke free from it, and pointed to a shining future.

So there we were, marooned in this unformed fantasy, treading water, drowning but too polite to wave, about to sink into despair, when along came the war with lifelines for all. All our uncertainties of identity, dislocations, could be submerged in the common good, in opposing Evil – in full-blown, brass-band, spine-tingling, lump-in-throat patriotism.

My father, George, and his best friend Mac, were seventeen in 1914. They joined the East Surrey Regiment, which, for some bureaucratic reason, was diverted from France to India. His schoolfriends, and most of the boys he knew, became subalterns and were sent to France. Scarcely any of them came back.

11

Meanwhile young George, who looks fourteen rather than seventeen in that first proud photograph in army uniform, was commissioned, transferred to the Indian Army, and ended as a captain commanding Gurkhas. In a story he never tired of telling, this boy, who lived to see a man walk on the moon, rode into battle against the Turks with a drawn sword on an Arab mare: 'It was a suicide mission, a charge against a Turkish artillery position. We all had to write a last letter home.'

They found the Turks had withdrawn, and that was as close as he ever got to action, nor did he write further letters, a task he always left to my mother. He was never again required to draw his sword in anger and, of course, the letter was not sent to his doting mother who begged him to come home when the war ended.

He was offered a Regular Commission in the Indian Army and wanted to stay on. He was having what he would later come to recognize as the time of his life. While his peers perished in the mud of Flanders, he stuck pigs, played polo and fell in love with an Indian princess. From the stories he told of those times, one image lingers in my mind. 'When we were sleeping under canvas, an Indian servant would sit crosslegged in the tent and fan me all night. I became so accustomed to this flow of cool air that if he dozed off and stopped fanning, I would instantly wake up and give him a tongue lashing.' I wonder about the thoughts of that Indian of long ago, faithfully fanning the innocent, ignorant face of an English boy of nineteen, the two of them in a tent under the stars in a subcontinent so heavy with history and mystery of which my father knew little and cared less.

Apart from the stories, he brought back the usual elephant's foot umbrella stand and carved ivories, which were powerful icons for me as a child and spoke of exotic worlds beyond the confines of suburban London. He had an annual bout of malarial fever for many years, and I would stand at his bedside listening to his delirious ramblings in Hindustani – probably berating the man for not fanning him. As he tossed and turned, an occasional wave of oven heat would escape the bedcovers and its moist and musky smell seemed to me the real palpable India that had stayed with him and escaped like a genie from a bottle once a year into our semi.

Our house, straining for middle-class status, like most in the street, had a name on the gate: 'Bhim-tam'! I faithfully reproduced it on the set for the film without knowing or wishing to know what it meant. I harbour the romantic hope that he named the house for that Indian princess, but I fear it is just Hindi for 'Mon Repos' or 'Dun Roamin'.

George may have been unscathed by the war and untouched by India, but rude shocks awaited him back in Wimbledon when he finally and reluctantly returned in 1920.

My grandfather had inherited the prosperous family laundry and had stolen a march on his competitors by inventing the first washing-machine, a large hexagonal wooden drum with diagonal ribs that took over from lines of washerwomen at tubs. So successful was it that he began to manufacture the machine and sell it to other laundries. Horsedrawn vans delivered the laundry so substantial stables were kept; the horses were the only part of the business that interested my father. Since money was being made, and his every whim was met, fine horses were found for him, which probably stood him in good stead when it came to riding into battle and, indeed young George's promotions probably came in part from his prowess in the chukkers.

My grandfather was essentially a happy-go-lucky inventor, and, apart from making the washing-machine, had no interest in the laundry which he left to his mother to run. He devised complicated clockwork toys and started a factory to make them, but never put enough effort into their marketing. He told me with gleeful amusement how his famous washing-machine had helped secure him an army contract to wash blankets during the First World War. The laundry was overwhelmed by the ever-increasing volume of military blankets that arrived each day. He solved the problem by employing teams simply to shake out the blankets, fold them, and send them back. One day he was summoned and arraigned before the Quartermaster-General. He was charged with sending back the blankets – not properly dried! He was stripped of the contract and a heavy fine was imposed. He could so easily have proved his innocence to the lesser charge by admitting a greater one. 'It proves there is justice in this world,' he said, drawing a moral, 'you just have to hope it doesn't come your way too often.' And his laugh rang out. He could laugh anything off. He saw the world as a huge joke – he just could not take it seriously.

He was a compulsive spender and giver of gifts. His house was always full of friends and relations and within seconds of their arrival he would have demonstrated to them just how trivial were their troubles. It was a laugh full of music, like runs on a clarinet, not the explosive barking laugh that belonged to my other grandfather, but full of notes and tunes that could play all day without repetition. 'If you're having fun,' he confided, 'you've got them fooled.' Who were *they*, I wondered. 'You'll know them when you meet them,' he laughed. And not too many years later I met them and knew them. He did allow himself the occasional serious interlude. He would take me aside and extract a solemn undertaking: 'Promise me you'll never wear anything but silk next to your skin,' or 'Never eat salmon unless it's smoked.' And this during wartime austerity.

One day my grandfather found himself in a train compartment sitting opposite a young widow. She was in great distress. She had been left penniless and was obliged to go into domestic service. Having lost her husband, she was now having to give her three-year-old son for adoption.

Grandfather told her she was too distressed to take such a decision. He had a son of the same age. 'You go and take up your position and I'll look after the boy until you get settled.' Grandma was quite accustomed to her husband arriving home with chance acquaintances who would stay for weeks at a time, and took it in her stride. The widow would visit on her day off, and the boy was brought up as my father's brother, went to public school with him and was married out of my grandparents' house, yet no formal arrangement was ever made. If the subject was raised, Grandpa would laugh it away. The young widow became a midwife and we always called her 'Nursey'. She was one of many who were simply always there on Sundays at Grandpa's.

However, when father returned from India, the laundry was

gone, the horses and land were lost, and the solid Victorian villa sold up. All that was left was a 'Trading Company', a yard full of junk: items that chums had left as security against loans from Grandpa; he was the softest touch. Even a little legacy my father had entrusted to Grandpa had melted away.

George, whose every boyhood desire had been met by an adoring mother, an indulgent father and the largesse of the family business, fawned upon and celebrated in India, an India in which he yearned to remain, came home to ruin and penury. Grandpa never explained, dismissed it with a peal of laughter. It was simply another joke: 'The joke's on me this time.'

When he died, he left nothing but his laughter ringing in our ears. I can hear it still. My sister's son Robert, whose birth is the climax of the film story that follows, inherited that clarinet laugh, in the way genes have of jumping generations. And, of course, the laugh is just the expression of an attitude. Robert can see the joke too. My father, however, could not, and iron entered his soul. Added to his private dismay was the public post-war catastrophe: a million servicemen thrown on to a depressed economy, many of them shell-shocked, wounded, crippled. I can recall as a child that if one went into the street or on a bus it was rare not to see an amputee. The year 1919 brought the pan-epidemic of influenza which killed more people than the war, some 20 million. Syphilis was rampant and incurable.

What Grandpa always had in abundance was friends. One of them was starting an oil company which became Shell-Mex. Grandpa told my father it was the coming thing and wangled him a job. 'The oil business is boring,' he used to say with glee, there being nothing like a good pun to get the tunes coming from the clarinet.

He kept right on inventing things. He made vacuum cleaners and rented them out by the hour, but at that time voltages varied from district to district and the motors kept burning out. I don't know what went wrong with his patent ice-cream machine. He told me it made ice-cream so delicious that children stole money from old women to buy it. There were even cases of kids clubbing their mothers to death when they were denied it. He had to stop making it, he said, before the country fell into anarchy.

My favourite was his Jack-in-the-box. You had to press certain spots in a particular order to get Jack to jump. You tried this, and tried that, the whole time in a state of unendurable apprehension, for at any moment, the silent, impenetrable box would burst open and Jack would leap out at you grinning and wagging on his spring.

Within a year of Grandpa's death his wife and daughter were comfortably provided for from bequests and gifts from some of that legion of friends he had helped in so many ways. When facing setbacks and reversals he would laugh it off with one of his best-loved invented clichés: 'It'll all turn out for the worst, so why worry?'

So my father had a job, but poor Mac just could not find one, even though he had left the army earlier than George. Most of their school friends had been killed in action, so George and Mac stuck together, were never apart. Word reached them that the new landlord of the Alexander Hotel at the foot of Wimbledon Hill had four beautiful daughters. When they got there it was jam-packed with young fellows come to worship at the shrine. Henry Chapman, eventually to become my Grandfather, had thoughtfully covered the walls behind the bars in mirrors. Only three of the daughters were in evidence, Bobby being still too young, but the reflections suggested an infinity of loveliness. They were innocent, demure. The mirrors caught their every movement, their graceful backs, their Lillian Gish profiles. My father, looking up, could observe the tops of their blonde heads floating in mirrors cunningly placed in the ceiling.

As George and Mac downed their pints of mild and bitter, swooning in that delirium of delight, they both fell in love with Ivy, the eldest of the Chapman girls. Each night they returned to gaze and eventually exchange a little badinage. One night the door of the pub burst open and there stood a striking figure in a long fur coat, smoking a cigar and flanked by two prize-fighters with cauliflower ears and potato noses. This was Ted Chapman, Grandpa's brother and deadly rival who owned the much larger and more fashionable hotel at the top of Wimbledon Hill, the Dog and Fox. Insults flew back and forth between the brothers and soon Ted was able to provoke an affray. George and Mac were quick to defend the honour of the house. How they welcomed the fists of the prize-fighters for the pain assuaged the greater agony of their unrequited love for Ivy. Soon they were to discover that the antagonism of the brothers was Sicilian in its tortured intensity. Ted's foray was a reprisal for a recent visit by Henry to the Dog and Fox that had climaxed in a lot of smashed glass and furniture. Henry had been registering his displeasure at Ted's attempt to lure his daughters to work behind *his* bars at the top of the hill. Henry's mirrors and daughters had severely dented Ted's takings. Furthermore, it seemed that Henry had taken the Alexander for the sole purpose of incommoding his brother. Their rivalry knew no bounds and no end: Ted's Rolls-Royce trumped Henry's Daimler; although Henry strongly disapproved of my father, he gave Ivy a lavish wedding since it had to be bigger than the one Ted gave his daughter.

In his later years Grandpa Henry left his wife for a woman who enshrined four of the attributes he most hated – she was a red-headed Irish Catholic barmaid. On his deathbed, he finally succumbed to her entreaties and a priest was called. He received a complete set of sacraments from baptism to extreme unction. The priest invited him to confess his sins, reminding him that he had lived a long and turbulent life, so he should take his time, look back carefully and remember as many of his misdeeds as he could. Henry racked his brains. 'I sometimes got angry, but I was always sorry afterwards. No. I can't think of anything at all.' Then a light came into his watery eyes. He spoke urgently into the priest's inclined ear, 'But I've got a rogue of a brother.'

George and Mac courted Ivy, took her out, were invited to the bungalow on the Thames at Shepperton that Grandpa Chapman kept as his weekend retreat. She was attracted to them both. She found it hard to separate them in her heart. Her father glowered disapproval. Neither was grand enough for his beautiful daughter. Just penniless opportunists, he told Ivy, but she was inclined to escape her overbearing and tyrannical father. She and her sisters had spent an incarcerated childhood in a gin palace, the Kingsbridge Arms, on the Isle of Dogs in the heart of London's dockland. Nannies and tutors tended to the four girls, but they scarcely left the fortress that blazed with light and the promise of oblivion in cheap gin or porter. Outside it was dangerous, dirty, brutish. This was before the First World War. Grandpa Chapman owned the only car in the area, a Unic. Mother remembers the swarms of barefoot urchins that would pursue them as they came and went. Some of them would leap on to the running board and Grandpa would swat them off. So isolated were they that my mother was seven years old before she realized that other people's parents did not drink a half-bottle of champagne for breakfast each morning. She told how they would pump hundreds of pints, which would then be lined up on the bars. As the hooter signalled the short midday break for the dockers, the doors to the pub would be flung open and the men would surge in, throwing a shower of pennies over the counter and grabbing their beers. After the rush, the pennies were swept up from the floor and set out in neat piles of twelve and columns of twenty.

Then came the war. Mother often vividly described watching the Zeppelins winding their stately way up the Thames, navigating by it. As each one reached its dockland target the gargantuan dirigible would drop a tiny little bomb. With casualties and damage all around them, Henry decided it was time to evacuate his young daughters. As a child, son of an East End coachman, he and his brothers were mudlarks playing and scavenging at the river's edge. Further up the Thames, in the rural middle reaches, prospering merchants and tradesmen were building riverside bungalows as weekend retreats. The motor car put it within reach. India was the influence and they built in the style of Simla or, most particularly, Kashmir – verandas with fretted decorative woodwork set up on stilts against flooding. Henry bought one (or perhaps built it) on Pharaoh's Island, which divides the river just above the lock at Shepperton. The particular conceit of this community was that each bungalow would be named for things Egyptian – there was a

Sphinx, a Pyramid, and so on. Grandpa's was called 'Philae'. So my mother and her sisters were taken to the riverside to escape a war, just as she would flee there with her children in the war that followed twenty years on.

When my father arrived on the scene, 'Philae' had been exchanged for 'Chestnuts' on the towpath – the Unic for a Daimler, the Kingsbridge Arms for the 'Alex' in Wimbledon.

George did not impress at rowing or punting, but he was a strong swimmer, which scored him some points. It was about this time that my mother's affections began to veer towards Mac, but Mac still had no job and so could make no offer. He loved her deeply, but felt obliged to step back and give his friend George a clear field. My father would turn up at Shepperton without him. George made the running and Ivy waited in vain for Mac to declare himself.

Meanwhile, Grandpa was doing his best to marry off his daughters to better men. He took them all to Ascot, completing his party with the Mayor of Wimbledon and other dignitories. With a wife and four daughters there were so many hats to buy and so much wrangling over prices and models that he bought a hat shop and bade them run it – which they did – into insolvency.

It was the twenties. George took Ivy to the *Danse de Thé* where her eyes would search for Mac – who was never there. Mother and her sisters were great exponents of the Charleston. They had river parties with several punts tied together, a wind-up gramophone and illumination by Chinese lanterns. There were regattas, leading up to Henley. They became flappers, cut their hair short. There were eligible young men, endless parties, it was gay, gay, gay. Above and beyond all else was the passion for river life and their contempt for stuffy conventional living.

My earliest memories, in the extreme close-up vision of infancy, are of the sheen of varnished boat mahogany, green-tinged brass fittings, the ring of wind-chimes, the addictive tang of creosoted wood, and my grandfather, an ogre in rope-soled canvas shoes, padding and pacing his veranda, the floorboards squealing under foot like squashed mice. Raised voices.

Thames-side revels, with my grandfather pouring champagne, my Aunt Jenny (Faith) holding the tambourine, below her my Aunt Billy (Hope), my father, George (Clive) pouring champagne for my grandmother.

My Aunt Billy (Hope) and my father George (Clive) sitting on my grandfather's Daimler.

My father white-faced, trembling. Mother snatching me away from contemplation of those textures, the taste of mother's tears mingling with the consoling smell of the pleated leather car seats on the way home. There is a photo of me at six months, sitting naked on a chocolate box, the picket gate of 'Chestnuts' in the background. The picture has been hand-tinted by Aunty Billy, the third Chapman sister.

It was almost certainly a row about money. After giving a lavish wedding Grandpa would have nothing more to do with Ivy and George, certainly not to alleviate their poverty. Father toiled at the clerical job he hated. Mother felt trapped in Rosehill Avenue. She pined for the river; my father's pleasure was the sea. As a bachelor he and his pals would race their belt-drive motorbikes down the Brighton Road. Now he liked to follow the same beloved route in his gleaming Austin 8 with wife and three children. Mac was married too, now, and ran a slightly superior, Union-Jack flying, Standard 10. He was doing well. His son was my best friend.

Mac and George would race their cars down the Brighton Road as they once had raced their motorbikes. 'They need a run down to Brighton for a good blow,' Dad would declare. This was his panacea for all ills, especially hacking coughs and running noses. 'A good blow' meant striding along the promenade taking deep breaths of the icy wind with its cutting edge of salt stinging our scabby noses. This cure-all air was 'ozone'. It was the patent medicine of 'Dr Brighton'. 'Bright, Brighter, Brighton,' ran the advertisement – perfectly expressing my father's philosophy. Of course, it was all to do with escaping the horrendous pall of coal pollution that hung over London and engulfed our sunny suburbs. Combined with the heavy mists of the low-lying Thames Valley, it produced those sickly yellow 'pea-souper' fogs. So we would lean into Brighton's 'ozone', a thirty-mile-an-hour wind that would 'flush out' the bad air, and 'blow through' us. The cleansing of the lungs was, if possible, extended to a purging of the flesh by a plunge into 'the briny'. My father would lead us into the surly grey sea. The angry waves dashed irritably at the pebbles and sent them, foam-borne, to pummel our pale and skinny flesh. This was the regimen, even in winter, and was known as 'a quick dip'.

Mother, on the other hand, always longed for the river, more particularly the Thames at her beloved Shepperton, and so we children were shuttled from one to the other, each parent extolling the virtues of river or sea. It took my father's absence in the army and a few well-aimed bombs for my mother to make her escape back to Shepperton and the river. In the last years of his life my father wrested back the initiative and bought a bungalow by the sea near Brighton. In his late seventies he still took regular 'quick dips' and went for his daily 'blow' along the front, although he began to remark that the tides were becoming 'most irregular' and were rushing in and out at shorter and shorter intervals. One day he looked up as a gull perched halfway up the sheer face of the chalk cliffs. 'That bird is in a very precarious position,' he remarked.

He would glare at the English Channel: 'The sea is our destiny.'

'In what way?' I asked.

'In every way. Atlantic convoys, the Armada, fish and chips.'

After he died my mother sold up and went to live in a flat facing the Thames at Kingston. She lives there still with her sister Jenny and just round the corner from the other two, Bobby and Billy. Mother at eighty-six is the eldest. They have all buried their husbands except Jenny, who spurned the institution of marriage. They love to picnic by the river in their many favourite places that recall girlish escapades. On a warm day they still like to slip into the water and swim across and back.

The four of them were frequent visitors to the set during filming. Early on I invited them to lunch at Bray Studios where I was rehearsing the actors. They were thrilled with Ian Bannen who was playing their father, calling him Dadda, and airing their grievances against him, encouraging him, correcting his clothing, his manner, his way of speaking. My mother was confronted by David Hayman, who is cast as her husband. He has a strong physical resemblance to my father, uncannily so, but my mother was not satisfied. 'He won't do,' she pronounced. 'George was much more handsome than that.' On the other hand, Derrick O'Connor, playing the role of her husband's best friend Mac, the man she loved all her life, is quite unlike the prototype. Nevertheless, she became quite flushed and skittish when she faced him. Derrick is the sort of man, my wife says, to whom women feel compelled to confess. Soon she was saying things to him, things she wished she had said to that other man, things that perhaps she had said over only in her thoughts.

Sarah Miles plied her with questions about her marriage, her sex life. Mother retreated skilfully into the vagueness that is the only toll eighty-six years have taken on body and mind. 'She has such a light in her eyes,' said Sarah. 'She has been strong and capable all her life, yet she has never lost her romance.' She reminded Sarah so much of her own mother.

Ivy still keeps up a prodigious correspondence. She writes vividly and cogently, but is plagued by lapses of memory. She did not forget to send me a Christmas card this year, but she forgot that she had not forgotten, and I received four cards on successive days.

As she and her sisters wandered about the sets of Rosehill Avenue, she was once again among the familiar possessions she had lost by fire. In her father's Shepperton bungalow, which I reconstructed in exact detail by the river's edge, she moved easily and happily back into her childhood. In old age the landscape of the past becomes clearer as the present mists over. She was able to revisit that past and touch it and the remembrances that now occupy so much of her mind took on substance and form. She and her sisters visited their past and it pleased them.

Chamberlain's speech announcing the onset of the Second World War is the beginning of the film. I remember every detail of that hour and have tried to render it in the scene. For both my parents it represented the possibility of deliverance. My father had lived a twenty-year hangover from the intoxication of his Indian Army days. Although he was nearly forty, he could not wait to join up. It was a blessed escape from the dull drudgery of his clerical job and perhaps vague and unformed dissatisfactions with his marriage and his street.

My mother found herself trapped in that suburban street, exiled from her beloved Thames and married to a man she was deeply fond of, but did not love. The friendly bombs fell and she gathered up her children and fled to Shepperton. My father begged his friend Mac to watch over us.

My mother did part-time war work in Mac's factory. He was an important man in a reserved occupation. He had a petrol allowance. He used to drive her home each afternoon. He would park his car by the river in front of our bungalow and I would see them talking, mute behind the glass, their long-dormant love blossoming – but, I suspect, not flowering.

Meanwhile I was immersed in the enchanted river-world of my mother's childhood. I swam and fished and became skilful in handling all manner of boats, skiffs, punts and canoes. My whole life was the river, in it, on it, by it, of it. One day I fell into the water just above the lock. The sluice gates were open and I was sucked down and, as hard as I fought, I could not regain the surface. The lock-keeper was afraid to close the sluices in case I was trapped in one of them and I had no choice but to hold my breath and wait for the lock to fill. I let the air escape. The body commands its functions: involuntarily I sucked in water, in and out. It made a roaring noise in my ears like the sound of the weir. I opened my eyes and watched the turbulent green water with considerable pleasure. I stopped struggling. I was breathing water, finally at one with the element I was so drawn to. I had become the river.

The lock-keeper fished me out with his boat hook and I spewed up the water from my stomach. The lungs clamp shut in such an emergency, I am told, and the body survives on what vestiges of oxygen remain in the system. I came back to consciousness with a nagging sense of regret, remembering the sublime harmony I had felt.

That river has flowed in my mind and memory all my life, a comfort, an inspiration and a consolation. The greatest satisfaction of this enterprise was to catch something of it on film.

The gaps in this narrative are occupied by the screenplay that follows.

Grandpa Chapman (*standing*), my mother (Ivy), Grandma, Jenny (*standing*),
Billy and Bobby seated, outside the Shepperton Thames-side bungalow (1916).

Me, my father, mother, sister Angela, at the Shepperton bungalow we moved to
after the bombing (1946).

The four Chapman sisters (1916), *left to right:* Ivy, my mother, rowing (Grace); Jenny (Faith); Billy (Hope); Bobby (Charity).

The four Chapman sisters (1946), *left to right:* Ivy, my mother, rowing (Grace); Aunt Jenny (Faith); Aunt Billy (Hope); Aunt Bobby (Charity).

Playing three of the sisters, *left to right*: Amelda Brown (Hope); Katrine Boorman (Charity); Jill Baker (Faith).

Hope and Glory

'Come, friendly bombs and fall on Slough'
John Betjeman

Hope and Glory was first shown in London on 3 September 1987.

The cast included:

BILL	Sebastian Rice Edwards
SUE	Geraldine Muir
GRACE	Sarah Miles
CLIVE	David Hayman
DAWN	Sammi Davis
MAC	Derrick O'Connor
MOLLY	Susan Wooldridge
BRUCE	Jean-Marc Barr
GRANDFATHER GEORGE	Ian Bannen
GRANDMA	Annie Leon
FAITH	Jill Baker
HOPE	Amelda Brown
CHARITY	Katrine Boorman
CLIVE'S PAL	Colin Higgins
WVS WOMAN	Shelagh Fraser
HEADMASTER	Gerald James
TEACHER	Barbara Pierson
ROGER	Nicky Taylor
ROGER'S GANG	Jodie Andrews
	Nicholas Askew
	Jamie Bowman
	Colin Dale
	David Parkin
	Carlton Taylor
PAULINE	Sara Langton
JENNIFER	Imogen Cawrse
MRS. EVANS	Susan Brown
LUFTWAFFE PILOT	Charley Boorman
POLICEMAN	Peter Hughes
HONEYMOON COUPLE	Ann Thornton
	Andrew Bicknell
PIANIST	Christine Crowshaw
CANADIAN SERGEANT	William Armstrong
FIREMAN	Arthur Cox

Writer/Director/Producer	John Boorman
Co-Producer	Michael Dryhurst
Director of Photography	Philippe Rousselot
Production Designer	Tony Pratt
Costume Designer	Shirley Russell
Editor	Ian Crafford
Sound Editor	Ron Davis
Music Composer and Conductor	Peter Martin
Casting	Mary Selway

1 . INT. ROHAN HOUSE: BACK GARDEN. SEPTEMBER 1939.
DAY
Colour.
*Raking down a line of suburban gardens lit by a late-summer sun.
Heads move back and forth above the fences that divide the narrow
strips of land, moving to the sound of unseen lawn mowers.*
   In one of these gardens two children, BILL *(aged eight) and his
sister* SUE *(aged six) disport themselves. They are sprawled out on
the lawn, heads and hands intent on something hidden from view in
the lush vegetation of a rockery garden. Beneath those flowers and
plants is a dark mysterious forest, shaded by huge leaves, and broken
up by towering boulders. Mounted figures of medieval knights ride
in, guided by* BILL'*s gigantic hand. A wizard appears in the path of
the riders who draw up sharply.* BILL *gives an impression of
neighing horses.* SUE'*s face looms up between large leaves. She
makes the sound of a spooky wind.*

2 . INT. ROHAN HOUSE: DINING/LIVING ROOM. DAY
In the penumbra of the room, the mother, GRACE, *in droopy
flowered frock, crosses, floats towards the walnut wireless and, with
trembling hand, switches it on. Its green dial glows with stations like
Droitwich and Hilversum. She glides back and drapes herself
behind an armchair in which her husband,* CLIVE, *sits solemn and
motionless.*

3 . EXT. ROHAN HOUSE: GARDEN. DAY
The sound of the lawn-mowers ceases abruptly. BILL *looks up
sharply. The neighbours' heads come to rest on top of the garden
fences. They turn, listening.* BILL *inclines his head towards the
french windows, sensing the dread moment. He walks towards the
door and is framed there. He regards his parents.*

4. INT. ROHAN HOUSE: DINING/LIVING ROOM. DAY

They look back with unseeing, inward-turned eyes. Young BILL
gathers confused fragments of the fateful announcement.

CHAMBERLAIN: (*Voice over*) . . . those assurances . . . by
eleven o'clock . . . a state of war . . . that this country . . .
at war with Germany.

(*The boy catches his mother's eye. She smiles an embarrassed
smile. The boy is embarrassed by her embarrassment. His
father's glassy solemnity angers him. In the garden,* SUE *sings.*)

SUE: (*Singing, out of shot*) Flat foot floogie with a Floy Floy,
Flat foot floogie with a Floy Floy.

(BILL *turns to his sister.*)

BILL: Stop that, Sue!

(CLIVE *is startled out of his funereal reverie.*)

She just sings it. She doesn't even know what it means.

(*An older sister,* DAWN, *a tumescent fifteen, stumbles into the
room in a nightdress.*)

DAWN: Where are my stockings? I can't find my stockings!

(*Her mother,* GRACE, *interrupts her with outstretched arms.*)

GRACE: Dawn, darling. They've started a war again.

(GRACE *says it as though announcing that dinner is served, but her voice is torn by a sob as she holds* DAWN *in her arms.*)

(*Whispering and sobbing*) We mustn't frighten the little ones.

(DAWN *is appalled by her mother's display of sentiment. She wrenches free.*)

DAWN: I don't care! I want my stockings!

(CLIVE *gets up, blazing. He seizes* DAWN *and shakes her.*)

CLIVE: Stockings? War! Don't you understand! War!

DAWN: I don't care!

CLIVE: War! War!

(GRACE *inserts herself between them.*)

GRACE: Clive. Don't. Dawn, please.

5. EXT. ROHAN HOUSE: GARDEN. DAY

BILL *calls out from the garden. He is jumping up and down, pointing at the sky.*

BILL: German planes! German planes!

(*They run out.* GRACE *sweeps little* SUE *into her arms, burying her face in her bosom and rushing back into the shelter of the house.* DAWN *and* CLIVE *scan the sky for planes. There are none.*)

I did see them. I did.

DAWN: He's the worst liar.

(DAWN *swings a fist at* BILL *and chases him into the room, raining savage blows upon him.*)

6. INT. ROHAN HOUSE: DINING/LIVING ROOM. DAY

Father is white with rage. He seizes them, one in each hand. Mother cowers with SUE.

CLIVE: These are the fruits of my loins?

BILL: I thought I saw them.

(DAWN *lunges at* BILL. *The* GRANDMOTHER *enters, tall, frail, elegant, ga-ga, deaf.*)

GRANDMA: Is it peace in our time?

GRACE: (*Shouting*) No, Mother! It's War! War!

35

GRANDMA: Or what?

GRACE: War! War! War!

(*The wireless begins to play 'God Save the King'. Father immediately lets go of the children and stands rigidly to attention. The others simmer down and shuffle into stiff and still poses.* GRANDMOTHER, *who perhaps cannot hear the Anthem, is baffled, shakes her head.*)

7. EXT. ROSEHILL AVENUE. DAY

The sirens sound. A shocking blast of noise, the sickening ululations of the air-raid warning. They call out over the rows of bow-fronted semi-detached, lower-middle-class suburban houses. Some of the occupants, more daring or more confused than their neighbours, burst out of their front doors, turning in frenzied circles, craning at the heavens.

8. INT. ROHAN HOUSE. DAY

The rigid family once more jerks into movement at the sound of the siren, looking fearfully out of the french windows, hiding under the table, clutching each other. The siren stops. They wait, anxiously. Silence. Even the birds stopped singing at the wailing of that first siren. This was perhaps the worst moment of the war, the first moment, when war was still an unknown dread thing. The siren again, but this time, a long sustained note.

CLIVE: That's the all-clear. Testing. They were just testing.

9. EXT. ROHAN HOUSE: GARDEN. DAY

CLIVE *walks tentatively into the garden, looking up, shielding his eyes against the sun. The others join him, one by one.*

GRACE: Such a beautiful day, too.

(*All search the clear blue sky. The sound of the lawn-mower starts up again where it left off before the war.*)

SUE: (*Singing*) Flat Foot Floogie with a Floy Floy.

10. INT. CINEMA. DAY

Black and white.

A Ministry of Information film advises and demonstrates how to glue strips of paper to windows to avoid flying glass, and how to construct an air-raid shelter. On the soundtrack, in addition to the patronizing commentary voice, is the sound of hundreds of screaming children.

BILL *and* SUE *sit among the children's matinée audience. The children pay no attention to the screen, but fight and shout, throw things at each other, jump over the seats, cry, wander up and down the aisles.*

The soundtrack changes to dramatic music and a transformation takes place. All movement and talking ceases. Hundreds of rapt faces stare at the screen where Hopalong Cassidy rides into action.

11. EXT. ROHAN HOUSE: GARDEN. DAY
Colour.

CLIVE *has put an Anderson shelter at the end of the small garden. He is shovelling earth on to its humped corrugated metal roof. His friend,* MAC, *is watching him.*

CLIVE: Going to put a rockery garden over it, Mac.

(BILL's *voice echoes from the inside of the shelter.*)

BILL: (*Out of shot*) Dad. It's full of water again.

(CLIVE *and* MAC *peer in to see the boy splashing up and down, water over his ankles. He clutches his submerged foot in mock agony.*)

Crocodiles! Aah!

CLIVE: The sodding water table.

MAC: Could you seal it over with hot pitch, Clive? Caulk it like the hull of a ship.

CLIVE: (*Caustic*) Thanks. I hope you can come for the launching.

12. INT./EXT. ROHAN HOUSE: KITCHEN/GARDEN. DAY
The windows are criss-crossed with brown paper. Beyond, in the garden, MAC *has taken off his jacket and is shovelling earth on to the shelter.* BILL *walks barefoot towards the house, carrying his wet socks and shoes in his hands.*

MOLLY: It's not fair on them. It's selfish to keep them with you.

GRACE: My aunt in Australia has offered . . .

(BILL *sits on the steps at the half-open kitchen door and wrings the water from his socks.* SUE *comes in and* GRACE *signals* MOLLY *to be circumspect, but she blunders on.*)

MOLLY: Snap it up. Great chance for them. Lot more future out there.

(BILL *listens, taking it all in.* GRACE *watches little* SUE *waddle out carrying plates.*)

GRACE: It's so far away. I couldn't bear it.

MOLLY: Kids don't care. You're thinking of yourself.

(GRACE *turns away, fighting back tears.* MOLLY *impulsively takes* GRACE *in her arms.*)

I didn't mean it like that, Grace. Why does it always come out wrong?

GRACE: I know you mean well.

(MOLLY *laughs and holds her at arms' length.*)

MOLLY: There you go again. You're so bloody nice. I want to shake you.

(*She does. Mock serious.*)

GRACE: Nothing will ever be the same again, Molly. And the funny thing is, I'm glad.

(MOLLY *looks at her, surprised.*)

MOLLY: Now you're talking.

SUE *listening to this, sees* BILL *on the steps and gives him a questioning look. He shrugs, trying to conceal his anxiety from his sister.*)

13. INT. ROHAN HOUSE: DAWN'S BEDROOM. DAY
DAWN *lies in bed, head buried in pillows in that deepest of all sleep, the Sunday morning adolescent lie-in.* BILL *shakes her, jumps on top of her, imitates an air-raid warning, tries to pull off the bedclothes, but she holds them tight.*
BILL: There's a soldier at the door, looking for you.
   (*She whips back the sheet, wide awake. One look at his face is enough to see that he is lying.*)
DAWN: You're the biggest fibber.
BILL: It's dinnertime. It really is. Cross my heart.
   (*She snakes out an arm and pulls him into bed. She rolls on top of him, tickling him and smothering him with kisses.*)
DAWN: If there's no soldier, I'll have you instead.
   (*He giggles and struggles, gets into a panic, but she merciless, won't stop. Finally he starts to cry. She leaps out of bed, disgusted with him.*)
Cry Baby Bunting.

14. INT. ROHAN HOUSE: GRACE'S BEDROOM. DAY
CLIVE *rummages in the wardrobe, chuckling to himself. He finds his Sam Browne belt and Army cap from the First World War.*

15. INT. ROHAN HOUSE: LIVING ROOM. DAY
MOLLY *and* GRACE *and* GRANDMA *have 'gin and its', the men, brown ale. They are in high spirits.* SUE *is doing a puzzle on the floor.* MOLLY *shouts into* GRANDMA's *ear.*
MOLLY: Few bombs might wake up this country.
   (GRACE *fills* MAC's *glass in a tender gesture. A look passes between them.* MOLLY *is a friend and a wife; they love and suffer in common.* DAWN *appears, wearing a defiant slash of lipstick.*)
GRACE: I doubt if a few bombs would wake up Dawn on a
   Sunday morning.
DAWN: This phoney war gets on my nerves. If we're going to
   have a war, I wish they'd get it started.
GRACE: Just ignore her, Mac.
   (CLIVE *appears having stripped to the waist but wearing his Sam Browne from the First World War. They all shriek with*

39

laughter. CLIVE, *encouraged by this response, does drill
movements and then demonstrates how to salute.*)
CLIVE: There are many ways of saluting. (*Demonstrates.*) An old
soldier insulting a young subaltern.
(*His hand flies to his forehead, gouging the air, the salute
transformed into an obscene gesture. More laughter.*)
As an officer, you counter that with one of these.
(*He raises his arm slowly and languidly until his limp hand just
brushes his temple. A faraway look in his eyes disdains any
acknowledgement of the insulting salute. A tiny skirmish in the
class war.* BILL *and* SUE *swing on the leather straps of the Sam
Browne. They want him to stop. They sense something
dangerous, alien, their father in an unfamiliar role, another
person. The wireless has been on all this time, playing music
and now come the chimes of Big Ben. It is news time. The
adults are suddenly stock-still and serious, leaving the children
stranded in an excited state.*)
NEWSREADER: (*Voice over*) Here is the news and this is Alvar
Lidell reading it.
(*The children are told to be quiet. The room becomes a frieze of
portentous concentration.*)

16. EXT. ROHAN HOUSE: GARDEN. DAY
BILL *slips out into the garden, looks up at a leaden sky imploringly.*
BILL: Come on. Come on.
(*The news bulletin filters out into the garden. Norway has
fallen, perhaps, or Churchill become Prime Minister.*)

17. INT. ROHAN HOUSE: DINING ROOM. DAY
*The meal has been eaten. They are animated again, but more
reflective.* DAWN *is winding wool with* GRANDMA. BILL *and* SUE
have also left the table. BILL *is looking at the Sam Browne, now
slung over an armchair, with its tangy smell and deep polish like
shiny milk chocolate, a mysterious icon of war. The conversation at
the table drifts over to him.*
MAC: . . . It was a toss-up. His company went to India, mine
went to France. Flip of a coin.
CLIVE: . . . two Indians to fan me all night. The heat.

40

MAC: . . . buried in a shell-hole for three days, while he's out there playing polo and sticking pigs.

GRACE: It was the best time of his life.

MAC: How many of our class left? You and me out of twenty-eight.

CLIVE: And Jim.

MAC: What's left of him. He'll never see the outside of the Star and Garter.

(BILL *sinks his teeth into the Sam Browne. He bites hard and is pleased to see that his teeth marks go quite deep into the leather.*)

CLIVE: I rode into battle . . .

(DAWN, *winding wool, knows this speech by heart and mimes it silently with her father.*)

. . . on horseback, with a drawn sword, leading a battalion of Gurkhas against the Turks.

(GRANDMA *watches* DAWN's *moving lips and strains to hear.*)

GRANDMA: I can't hear you.

MOLLY: And where were the Turks?

(*She also knows the story.*)

GRACE: No Turks.

CLIVE: We didn't know that. It was a suicide mission. Machetes against artillery. Volunteers only.

GRACE: They'd gone.

MOLLY: Saw Clive coming.

(*They all have a good laugh at* CLIVE's *expense and he takes it well enough.* BILL *drifts over to his lead soldiers spread out in a corner of the room. They are an eclectic mix of cowboys, Indians, the medieval knights, as well as modern militia and a few farm animals.*)

CLIVE: We all had to write a last letter home.

GRACE: And it was the last. Hasn't written a letter since. Not even a birthday card.

(BILL *sets a mounted knight against a clutch of modern infantry.*)

MAC: It's not like that when you're in it. Just young boys spilling their guts in the mud.

DAWN: What were they like, the Germans, when you were a

prisoner-of-war?

(BILL *looks up with interest. The others fall silent.*)

MAC: Most of them were very decent to me.

MOLLY: I wish you wouldn't go saying that. You'll get into trouble.

DAWN: You can speak German, can't you?

MAC: A bit.

DAWN: Say something. I want to know what it sounds like.

MOLLY: Certainly not!

MAC: In den ganzen Welt die meisten Leute sind dumm.

MOLLY: Not so loud!

18. INT. ROHAN HOUSE: DINING ROOM. DAY

Later. The two men are in post-prandial sleep in the armchairs on either side of the fire. Sounds of washing up and women's voices come from the kitchen. BILL *walks up very close and examines these two warriors from the Great War, or the First World War, as it was now coming to be known. Their mouths are open, slack. His father's false teeth click up and down as he breathes.* MAC *shifts his backside in his sleep to let a fart up from the side of the leatherette armchair.* BILL *looks at* CLIVE's *mottled skin, the stubble, the sagging epidermis around the eyes. He goes to the mantelpiece and takes down a silver-framed picture of his father as a baby-faced second lieutenant wearing that same Sam Browne.* BILL *holds the picture next to his father's snoring face. Once again, a news bulletin begins on the ever-playing wireless.*

BILL: Dad, the News. It's the News.

(CLIVE *stirs.*)

CLIVE: Go off and play, son.

(BILL *shakes him.*)

BILL: But Dad, it's the News.

CLIVE: Thanks, son. I can hear it. I'm not sleeping, just closing my eyes.

(BILL *is confused. He still feels it is his duty to wake him.*)

BILL: (*Shouting*) The Germans! They've landed!

(GRACE *and* MOLLY *appear at the door, alarmed. The men sleep on.*)

Only joking.

19. INT. ROHAN HOUSE: CHILDREN'S BEDROOM. NIGHT
BILL *and* SUE *are in two beds, side by side. Between them is a crystal set and they are sharing the earphones listening to* Itma *or* Much Binding in the Marsh. *Their door is half open and a gust of shouts and cries rises from below.* BILL *gets up and goes to the door.*

20. INT. ROHAN HOUSE: HALLWAY AND LANDING. NIGHT
BILL *and* SUE *venture out on to the landing and peer through the banisters to the hallway and front door below.*

21. INT. ROHAN HOUSE: HALLWAY. NIGHT
MAC *and* MOLLY *are leaving, as* CLIVE *and* GRACE *help them on with their coats. They have had a few more drinks, and are making sentimental farewells.* MOLLY *is sobbing uncontrollably.*
MOLLY: Bloody gin. Always makes me cry.

43

MAC: Got some wires crossed. Only weeps when she's happy.

GRACE: You're making me start now.

(*MAC embraces her.*)

MAC: Now, now, Grace.

(*He turns to* CLIVE *and takes him by the shoulders. They are both quite drunk.*)

Root it out. Clive . . . the thought of it, before it takes hold.

CLIVE: Weeds will grow, Mac.

MAC: Consider Grace, the kids. I love them like my own. And you.

CLIVE: Kiss me, Hardy.

(*As he mentions the children,* MOLLY *wails anew.*)

MOLLY: Why couldn't I have kids? Is He sitting up there . . .

(*She points upwards and* BILL *and* SUE *cringe back.*)

. . . saying, 'Grace, yes; Molly, no'?

(*GRACE holds her tight.*)

GRACE: Better off, Molly. What's to become of the poor mites!

(*SUE's face creases and tears well up.* BILL *puts a protective arm about her.*)

MAC: You're a mug, Clive. We did our bit in the Last Lot.

CLIVE: If King and Country call, Mac, you'll go as soon as I will.

(*MAC's face goes white with anger.*)

MAC: What did we know? We were seventeen.

CLIVE: (*With a far-off look*) I heard the drum and fife yesterday, Mac, marching past. Made my hair stand on end. I thought, I've been asleep for twenty years.

(*MAC wants to hit him. He turns away, trembling.*)

MAC: Go to hell.

(*He puts an arm about* MOLLY *and plunges into the blacked-out pitch-dark winter night. As* GRACE *turns back, she glimpses the children on the landing above.*)

GRACE: Do you know what time it is? Go back to bed, this instant.

(*They dart out of sight.*)

22. ROHAN HOUSE: CHILDREN'S BEDROOM. NIGHT

BILL *and* SUE *slide under the bedclothes.* SUE *is whimpering.*

44

BILL: We're not going to be like them when we grow up. We're
not even like them now.
*(He picks up the earphones and twiddles with the crystal
wireless. It is the News again.* BILL *fiddles with his lead
soldiers, his eyes getting heavy.)*

23. EXT. BATTLEFIELD. DAY
Black and white.
Infantry advance as shells burst all about them. CLIVE *and* MAC
push forward, side by side. MAC *is hit, goes down, cries out for help,
but* CLIVE *does not seem to notice.*
A muddy field. Silence. Aftermath of battle. BILL *searches
among the dead. They are half buried, covered in mud, all one
texture with the earth.* BILL *finds* CLIVE *and* MAC, *lying side by
side, dead. He is quite unconcerned, pulls at his father's Sam
Browne which slips off easily. He wipes the mud away and starts to
eat it. It seems to be made of chocolate.*

45

24. EXT. SUBURBAN STREET. DAY

Colour.

A 1938 Vauxhall 12 is parked outside a recruiting centre. A boisterous crowd of young men mills about, passing in and out, encouraging each other, cheering each new man who steps out a soldier. Next door is a pub and there is a continuous exchange of customers between the two establishments. BILL *and* SUE *wait inside the car. She is whining in the back, sucking her thumb.* BILL *sits in the driving seat, pretending to drive, making all the right noises.*

SUE: He's never going to come back. He's gone off to be a soldier and Mummy doesn't even know.

BILL: It doesn't matter, I can drive the car home.

SUE: You wouldn't.

BILL: Would.

SUE: You couldn't.

BILL: Could.

(CLIVE, *arm in arm with a* PAL, *comes out of the pub and over to the car. He gets in after much handshaking and back-slapping.*)

CLIVE Sorry, kids. Joined up. I needed some Dutch courage to tell your mother.

(*the* PAL *opens the passenger door and leans in.*)

PAL: Never say die!

CLIVE: Steady the Buffs.

PAL: Up the Arsenal!

(CLIVE *leans across and slams the door closed. The* PAL *waves in at the window.* CLIVE *pulls away. The* PAL *runs alongside, waving.* CLIVE *laughs and waves back.*)

CLIVE: He's one of the best.

(*Still the* PAL *keeps up with the car, running frantically.*)

SUE: Daddy you shut his hand in the door.

(*The* PAL *jumps on the running board and crouches there, red-faced, eyes bulging. He waves in desperately at the window.*)

CLIVE: The silly bugger.

(*He pulls up and opens the door. The* PAL *clasps his hand and writhes in agony.*)

You silly bugger. We're trying to win the war and you start off by shutting your fingers in the bloody car door.

25. INT. ROHAN HOUSE: GARAGE. DAY

CLIVE *is putting the car up on blocks, taking off the wheels.* BILL *helps him.*

CLIVE: That's it for the duration. (*Runs a duster lovingly over the bodywork.*) I shall miss the old girl. Pop in and give her a polish, Billy boy. Just now and then. A car needs to be cherished.

(GRACE *has appeared at the door and heard some of this.*)

GRACE: Has Sue got it right?

CLIVE: What's that?

GRACE: You joined up.

CLIVE: Oh, that.

GRACE: I wish you could have told me yourself.

(*He takes her in his arms.*)

CLIVE: Oh, Grace, it's not for long. They say it'll be over by Christmas.

(CLIVE *laughs and tickles her, trying to get round her, keep it light.* GRACE *laughs despite herself.* BILL *makes a face, disgusted by the show of sentiment.*)

GRACE: Don't be so daft. Act your age. (*Extricates herself, sighing.*) I can't cope on my own. I'd better let the children go.

26. EXT. ROHAN HOUSE: GARDEN. DAY

CLIVE *leads* BILL *out on to the lawn, goes down on one knee and puts his hand on the boy's shoulder. He looks solemnly into his son's eyes.*

CLIVE: Billy boy. Before I go, there's something I want to tell you. You're old enough now. It's time. (*Produces a cricket ball from his pocket.*) The googly. Your hand is too small to master it, but not to start practising. Anyway I'm going to pass on the secret now, father to son, in case anything happens to me. (*Demonstrates.*) You know the off-break, right?

(*He flicks the ball out of his wrist.* BILL *nods.*)

And the leg-break?

(BILL *knows that too. The ball comes out of the hand, spinning the other way.*)

Now, the googly looks like a leg-break, but it's really an off-break. Got it? Like this.

BILL: It's like telling fibs.

CLIVE: That's it. When you tell a lie, you hope to get away with it. When someone else does, you want to find them out. A good batsman will spot a googly. A good bowler will hide it. Always remember that, son.

(BILL *flicks the ball this way and that, experimenting.* CLIVE *watches him tenderly, a moment of perfect harmony. He folds* BILL *in his arms, holding him fast.*)

27. EXT. ROHAN HOUSE: FRONT DOOR. DAY

BILL *swings on the front garden gate looking back at his mother,* SUE *and* DAWN *bidding their farewells to* CLIVE *in a confusion of tears and forced gaiety.*

28. EXT. ROHAN HOUSE: FRONT GARDEN. DAY
CLIVE *finally strides away, head high, a military spring already in his step. Behind him* GRACE *shuts the door as though closing a chapter of their lives.*
BILL: Dad! Dad!
    (CLIVE, *now some twenty yards away, looks back.* BILL *throws the cricket ball and* CLIVE *catches it neatly. He smiles and marches off down Rosehill Avenue.* BILL *is puzzled as* CLIVE *shows no sign of returning the ball. He calls after him.*)
Dad!
    (CLIVE *is now eighty yards down the street. He suddenly turns, smiling broadly, and with a prodigious throw he sends the ball in a high arc towards his son.* BILL *juggles his position, cups his hands, gets under it as the hard, heavy ball hurtles downwards. At the last moment he loses his nerve and jumps back, letting the ball thump into the lawn. He looks towards* CLIVE, *full of shame.* BILL *is relieved to see that his father has turned the corner.*)

29. INT. ROHAN HOUSE: LIVING ROOM. DAY
BILL *winces as he and* SUE *are passed from hand to hand, hugged and kissed by the many female members of the family –* DAWN,

GRANDMA *and* GRACE's *three sisters,* FAITH, HOPE *and*
CHARITY. MOLLY *is on hand with* MAC, *the only male. On the*
table are the remains of the farewell party, an iced cake, balloons,
gaudy wrapping paper. Encouraging cries fly about: 'Aren't you
lucky?' 'Isn't it exciting?' 'I wish I could hide in your suitcase.'
From the smothering embraces, BILL *casts a pleading look to* MAC
who reaches out and hauls him from the women.
MAC: You survived that. The war should be no problem.
    (GRACE *ties a label to* BILL's *lapel. It declares his name and*
    other details.)
GRACE: Time to go.
    (*She leads the children out.* MAC *follows, carrying the two*
    suitcases.)

30. EXT. WATERLOO STATION. DAY
MAC *and* GRACE *lead* BILL *and* SUE *into the concourse where*
hundreds of children are assembled, each wearing an identification
label. The noise is overwhelming. The organizers shout into
megaphones. One boy has fainted and is put on a stretcher by St
John's Ambulancemen and, to get through the crowd, they hold the
stretcher above their heads. The boy recovers, sits up and waves to
his friends. The parents throng behind the barrier and the children
are penned in. MAC *pushes his way through and they follow him.*
WVS *Volunteers stand guard.*
WVS WOMAN: Australia?
    (GRACE *nods. The* WVS WOMAN *examines the labels on* SUE
    and BILL *and checks them against her list. The steam and noise*
    have a suffocating effect on GRACE.)
    Say goodbye and pass them through.
    (GRACE *weeps as she embraces* SUE. BILL *fights back the tears*
    and turns away embarrassed when his mother wants to kiss
    him.)
BILL: I'm going to miss the war and it's all your fault.
    (*They are sucked into the enclosure and quickly disappear*
    among the throng of refugee children. GRACE *tries to follow*
    them with her eyes, searching for them hungrily. They
    disappear. MAC *flinches at the pain he sees in her face. She*
    lunges forward, and tries to push through the barrier.)

GRACE: I can't do it. What's the point?

MAC: It's just the wrench, Grace. It's for their sake.

(*He tries to restrain her, but she breaks free.*)

GRACE: Let me through, I want my children.

WVS WOMAN: No one goes in there. You signed the forms, didn't you?

GRACE: Yes, I did. And now I want them back.

WVS WOMAN: Too late. Plenty of others would've been glad of their places.

(*The* WVS WOMAN *and an* ARP MAN *are forcibly holding her.* MAC *cannot bear to watch her pain. He leaps over the barrier, grabs* SUE *and* BILL *and hoists them out of the pen.* BILL *is acutely embarrassed at the scene his mother is making. He struggles to get free of* MAC.)

BILL: Let me alone. I want to go. I want to go.

(MAC *swings them over to* GRACE. *She snatches up* SUE *and hugs her. Over the child's shoulder her eye is drawn to a poster depicting a ghostly Hitler hovering over a mother and her children. He whispers in her ear, 'Take them back.'*)

In front of everybody. They were all looking at us. Why did you have to do it?

(GRACE *is shattered, drained. She becomes calm, almost dreamy.*)

GRACE: Please yourself. (*Turns to* MAC.) Let them go, if they want.

MAC: Grace!

(GRACE *turns back to the barrier, which is still defended by the* WVS WOMAN *with the clipboard.*)

WVS WOMAN: Changed your mind again?

GRACE: Yes, I have.

WVS WOMAN: Well, you're too late. Apply again. On your head be it.

31. INT. ROHAN HOUSE: LIVING ROOM. NIGHT

BILL *glues balsa-wood wings on to a model Spitfire. Opposite him, across the dining-room table,* GRACE *is cutting something out of the newspaper.* DAWN's *school books are spread out on the table, but she has abandoned them in favour of a dancing lesson by Victor*

52

Sylvester on the wireless. She steers her imaginary partner between the furniture, her face rapt with concentration, trying to follow the steps.

VICTOR SYLVESTER: (*Voice over*) Slow, quick, quick, slow. Right forward – left together – three, four – back together – turn – one, two – quick, quick, slow.

(GRACE *crosses the room towards the kitchen.* DAWN *passes in front of her and she falls into step partnering her daughter in the dance.*)

DAWN: You know it? It must be an old one.

GRACE: Ancient. Have you finished your homework?

DAWN: After this dance.

(*She mouths the steps, 'Forward – quick, quick, slow.'*)

32. INT. ROHAN HOUSE: KITCHEN. NIGHT
GRACE *pins the newspaper cutting to a bulletin board which also displays a 'war map' with pins in it showing the progress of hostilities. The cutting is a David Low cartoon showing a soldier standing defiantly on a rocky promontory looking across a stormy sea towards France, saying, 'Very well, alone.' She is deeply moved by it.* BILL *enters and watches her, sensitive of her mood, but he has a mournful duty. He takes out the pins representing the German army in Russia.*

BILL: I've got to move the Germans to Minsk. They've taken Minsk.

(GRACE *lays a restraining hand on his shoulder.*)

GRACE: Tomorrow. Give them one more night of freedom. Move them in the morning.

33. INT. ROHAN HOUSE: LIVING ROOM. NIGHT
Swirling to the dance music, DAWN *comes face to face with the clock on the mantelpiece and registers the hours. She dives for the wireless and searches for another station. She is satisfied when she hears the stentorian tones of Lord Haw-Haw's nightly propaganda broadcast from Germany.*

DAWN: Quick! Lord Haw-Haw! He's starting.

(BILL *scampers in.* GRACE *hovers by the door.*)

LORD HAW-HAW: (*Voice over*) . . . the soldiers like to wager
among themselves, what day will the German army enter
Moscow? One thing is certain: much sooner than anyone
thought. From here in Berlin, listeners in Britain, I can
give some very definite news. There will be a bomber raid
on London tonight, the fourteenth night in succession.
Look out for bombs if you live in Carshalton or Croydon.
There will be incendiary attacks if you live in Fulham and
Hammersmith. And watch out in Kew; be alert in
Walthamstow.
(BILL *looks back at his mother.* DAWN *gets up and goes over to
the wireless, staring at it.*)
BILL: That's us.
GRACE: It's just German propaganda.
DAWN: He always knows.
GRACE: Half the time he's bluffing.
(*A moment of dread hangs over the room.* GRACE *summons her
resolve and bustles over to the wireless and snaps it off.*)
Bill, off to bed.
(*She gives him a shove towards the door to silence his protest.
She takes* DAWN *by the shoulders and presses her into a chair
and pushes her head into her homework.*)

34. INT. ROHAN HOUSE: CHILDREN'S BEDROOM. NIGHT
*Sirens are sounding, one after another, some distant, some close, then
the one at the end of the street, like dogs howling in the night, waking
other dogs. Three German bombers, a Heinkel, a Dornier and a
Stuka, fly in formation against the black sky.* GRACE *appears
behind the model planes, which hang on threads from the ceiling,
wakes* BILL *and* SUE *and they stumble out of bed.*

35. INT. ROHAN HOUSE: STAIRS. NIGHT
GRACE *leads* BILL *and* SUE *down the stairs. They sleep on their feet
in this familiar routine.* DAWN *is still dressed below, playing dance
records on the gramophone and finishing her homework.*
GRACE: We'd best go to the shelter.

36. INT. ROHAN HOUSE: LIVING ROOM. NIGHT
They open the french windows and a fierce wind cuts into the room.

DAWN: It's freezing out.
(GRACE *hesitates, then closes the windows.*)

37. INT. ROHAN HOUSE: HALLWAY. NIGHT
They squeeze themselves into the tiny space under the stairs, close the door and light a candle. BILL *and* SUE *complain irritably as they try to arrange their limbs. The shoving and pushing wakes them up.* GRACE *gives each of them a biscuit from a tin.*
DAWN: What would we do if a German came into the house?
GRACE: Don't be silly, Dawn.
DAWN: Well, why do you always bring the carving knife in here?
(DAWN *picks up the knife, pretending to hear someone outside the cupboard door. She presses her ear to the thin wooden partition.* BILL's *eyes bulge. He is half convinced. Even* GRACE *looks uneasy.* SUE, *reacting automatically to crisis, pulls on her red and blue 'Mickey Mouse' gasmask. Suddenly* DAWN *thrusts the knife through a crack in the boards. She makes a blood curdling cry.*
Got him!
(GRACE *slaps her, amused, despite herself.* BILL *seizes* DAWN *from behind and pulls her back on top of him. They writhe and giggle.* BILL *cocks an ear.*)
BILL: Flak!
(*They are stock-still, straining to hear. He is right. The anti-aircraft guns have started up. Their crisp 'crump' sound gets closer and more frequent. Another separate sound intrudes – falling bombs. The explosions are at regular intervals, each one louder than the last.*)
Basket bombing. (*Counts between the bombs.*) Two and three and four and five and six and . . .
(*The next bomb falls closer.*)
GRACE: Why didn't I take you to the shelter?
(*Her hands touch and caress the children, as though weaving a protective charm over them.*)
BILL: . . . four and five and six and . . .
(*Another, louder still. They sit tense and straining every muscle, willing the bombs away.*)

55

GRACE: If only I'd let you go to Australia.

BILL: . . . and five and six and . . .

(*It is deafening, shaking the house.*)

DAWN: The next one is ours. Either it hits us or it goes past us.

BILL: . . . and four and five . . .

DAWN: Please God. Not on us. Drop it on Mrs Evans. She's a cow.

BILL: . . . and six . . .

(*It drops, some way past them. They slump exhausted against each other. A fire-engine bell approaches. The flak goes on. DAWN gets up, untangles herself from the others.*)

DAWN: I'm not going to die like a rat in a trap. Let me out of here. (*Staggers out of the cupboard.*) I'm going outside.

(BILL *scrambles after her.*)

GRACE: Wait. Don't.

38. EXT. ROHAN HOUSE. NIGHT

DAWN *runs out. Searchlights criss-cross the sky. Anti-aircraft shells make little white puffs in the black sky, the sound coming much later. Up the road, a house is blazing. A fire engine swings by. ARP men run in the street.* DAWN *dances in the tiny front garden.*

DAWN: Quick, quick – slow, quick, slow.

(BILL *hesitates in the porch.*)

It's lovely. Lovely. Does little Billy want to see the fireworks?

(BILL *runs out, sees something by the kerb and picks it up.*)

BILL: Shrapnel! And it's still hot.

(*He tosses it from hand to hand. At the far end of the street, the skyline of central London is silhouetted against a burning sky.* GRACE *suddenly laughs at the sight of the burning house down the street. She is shocked at her own reaction.*)

GRACE: Come in at once, or I wash my hands of you.

(*A shell bursts right overhead and they duck into the open doorway. The four of them are framed there, looking up at the savage sky where the Battle of Britain rages.* BILL *watches, enraptured.*)

39. EXT. THE CITY OF LONDON. NIGHT
Black and white.
St Paul's sits at the heart of the blazing city.

40. EXT. STREET. DAY
Colour.
DAWN, in school uniform, rides off on her bicycle. BILL and SUE come out with school satchels and gasmasks. GRACE watches them making their way along the street scarred and damaged by the night's bombing. People scratch in the rubble to salvage their belongings. BILL's eyes are fixed on the ground searching for shrapnel. Now and then he stops to retrieve a piece. SUE dawdles along behind him, one foot in the gutter, the other on the kerb.
   BILL looks up as he hears a voice groaning from a bomb site. SUE is now some way ahead. The street is suddenly deserted. He looks back at the bomb-scarred house. A bathtub is suspended dizzily by one leg from an electric cable. The front of the house is gone and flowery wallpapers are revealed. The voice cries out again, a panting, rasping moan. BILL ventures forward. Now a woman's voice, groaning.
MAN'S VOICE: Oh fuck . . . oh fuck . . . oh fuck . . .
   (A white hand and forearm stretch up from the debris. BILL shifts position until he can see two heads, a male and female, pressed against a mattress which is leaning against a broken wall. He darts back on to the street and looks for help. The street is still deserted. He hesitates, then runs up the street for all he is worth.)

41. EXT. SCHOOLYARD. DAY
BILL and SUE are late. They run into the yard where the other children are already lining up in their respective classes. The HEADMASTER is a wizened Welshman, too old for military service. He struts up and down.
HEADMASTER: Dressing from the right!
   (He points an accusing finger at BILL.)
Late! My study before prayers.
   (They shuffle into their correct spacing.)
Eyes front! Keep still down there, you little ones. It's

57

discipline that wins wars. (*Inspects his troops.*) Now quick
march. Left . . . right . . . left . . . right . . . Swing those
arms.

42. INT. HEADMASTER'S STUDY. DAY
Flash cut. BILL *flinches and winces as the cane strikes his hand.*

43. INT. SCHOOL ASSEMBLY HALL. DAY
*The children are praying, eyes closed, hands joined. On the dais, the
teachers, mostly women, are lined up.*
HEADMASTER: Oh God, bring destruction to our enemies.
    Make these young ones true soldiers of the Lord. Guide Mr
    Churchill's hand in the cunning of war.
    (*Some of the boys covertly swap pieces of shrapnel and cigarette
    cards as the* HEADMASTER'*s tirade grows in passion, but* BILL
    *is mesmerized and fearful of this daily rhetoric. He blows on his
    hands, shakes them to alleviate the pain inflicted by the
    caning.*)
    Let our righteous shells smite down the Messerschmitts
    and the Fokkers.

44. INT. HEADMASTER'S STUDY. DAY
Flash cut. BILL'*s face, twisted in anxious anticipation, awaits the
next blow.*

45. INT. SCHOOL ASSEMBLY HALL. DAY
HEADMASTER: Lord, send troublesome dreams to Herr Hitler.
    Let him not sleep the sleep of the innocent. And comfort
    our warriors at the fronts. Brighten their swords, burnish
    their bullets with your fire.

46. INT. HEADMASTER'S STUDY. DAY
Flash cut. BILL *jerks convulsively and grins as the cane connects.*

47. INT. SCHOOL ASSEMBLY HALL. DAY
The HEADMASTER *reaches a climactic peak, then is silent, head
sinking to his chest. He continues, very quietly.*
HEADMASTER: We beseech Thee, oh Lord, to have mercy on

these Thy children.

48. INT. HEADMASTER'S STUDY. DAY
Flash cut. BILL *suffers another whack.*

49. INT. SCHOOL ASSEMBLY HALL. DAY
HEADMASTER: We dedicate our studies this day to the war
   effort.

50. INT. CLASSROOM. DAY
BILL *covertly shows the welts on his hands to his neighbour as he
and thirty other nine-year-old children are harangued by a large red-
faced woman, their* TEACHER. *She sprays a lot of saliva as she
speaks. A coloured linen projection of the world is hung over the
blackboard. She slaps it with her cane, pointing to many countries.*
TEACHER: Pink . . . pink . . . pink . . . pink . . . What are the
   pink bits, Rohan?
   (BILL *stands up, still seeking balm for his hands – he has them
   tucked under his armpits.*)
BILL: They're ours, Miss.
TEACHER: Yes, the British Empire.
   (*A boy,* HARPER, *sits in the front row and is in saliva range.
   Each time the* TEACHER *turns back to the blackboard, the boy
   wipes his desk flamboyantly with a cloth, much to the
   spluttering amusement of his classmates.*)
   Harper, what fraction of the earth's surface is British?
HARPER: Don't know, Miss.
TEACHER: Anyone?
   (*A girl shoots up her hand.*)
   Jennifer Baker.
JENNIFER: Two-fifths, Miss.
TEACHER: Yes. Two-fifths. Ours. And that's what the war is all
   about. Men are fighting and dying to save all the pink bits
   for you ungrateful little twerps.
   (*The pinched little faces find this notion difficult to absorb.
   They stare back blankly at the British Empire. A siren sounds
   an air-raid warning.*)
   Books away! Scramble!
   (*They grab their gasmasks and run from the class, cheering.*)

59

51. EXT. SCHOOLYARD. DAY
The children swarm to the shelters, which are long narrow concrete structures covered in sandbags to absorb blast.

52. INT. SHELTERS. DAY
The children file in noisily, laughing and chattering. There are clattering duckboards on the ground affording cover from an inch or two of water. Along each side of the shelters are narrow benches. The children sit facing each other. The HEADMASTER's *steel-studded boots hammer noisily down the steps. He raises his arms high.*
HEADMASTER: Gasmasks on!
> *(They open up their cases and pull on their masks. The* HEADMASTER *conducts their breathing, moving his arms up and down to indicate the rhythm.)*
> Slowly . . . in . . . out . . . don't panic . . . in . . . out . . .
> *(There is a hissing sound as they inhale, then a rasping comic raspberry as the air is pushed out of the sides of the rubber masks where they meet the cheeks.)*
> In . . . out . . . These masks are given to us to filter away the abominations of the enemy.
> *(He marches up and down in the narrow gap between the scabby knees of the children.)*

Now, nine times table. One times nine is nine . . .
(*The children's muffled voices chant the multiplication table,
rubbery gurgling sounds emerge from the gasmasks. Hidden
behind his mask,* BILL *finally gives way to angry tears. He
sticks out his tongue as the* HEADMASTER *passes by.*)
Two times nine is eighteen . . .
(*And so on.*)

53. EXT. ROSEHILL AVENUE. DAY
BILL *and* SUE *turn into their street on their way home from school,
looking lifeless and dull, but their faces light up with excitement as
the fifty foot length of a barrage balloon suddenly rises from behind
the houses to the distant sound of cheering children. They sprint into
their house.*

54. INT. ROHAN HOUSE. DAY
BILL *and* SUE *run through the hallway and into the living room,
scattering satchels, hats, coats, gasmasks in their wake. Their
excitement is far too intense to explain to the startled* GRACE. *They
burst out through the french windows into the garden.*

55. EXT. ROHAN HOUSE: GARDEN. DAY
*They run to the back fence. In the waste ground beyond the garden,
where a further row of houses was to be built when war intervened,*
BILL *and* SUE *witness a team mostly of airwomen* (WRAFS) *intent
on launching the balloon. Some twenty women, each holding a
tether, are paying out their lines under the rhythmic commands of
their leader. There is a cable attached to the winch mounted on a
truck, and this is wound out as the balloon rises. The balloon has a
comforting, humorous aspect, and the children laugh and giggle as
they watch.*

56. NEWSREEL
Black and white.
   *Like a school of basking whales, barrage balloons fill the sky. It is
a newsreel of the Battle of Britain. A dramatic scene follows: a 'dog
fight' between Spitfires and German bombers. A patriotic, punning
commentary, pulsating music.*

57. INT. CINEMA. DAY
Colour.

GRACE and her three children are glimpsed in their seats, watching. BILL is totally engrossed, enthralled. Out of habit, he simulates the engine noise of the planes and the clatter of cannon fire. Suddenly a caption is superimposed on the screen: AIR RAID IN PROGRESS – YOU ARE ADVISED TO TAKE SHELTER. *GRACE leads them out. They shuffle up the aisle, dragging their feet, watching over their shoulders as they go.*

BILL: Can't we just see the end?

DAWN: They've got the real thing outside.

BILL: It's not the same.

58. EXT. ROSEHILL AVENUE. DAY
A number of people have come out of their suburban gardens and look up at the pale-blue winter sky. GRACE, SUE and BILL are among them. A squadron of Spitfires is attacking a formation of German bombers. They are distant black dots high above the barrage balloons. The planes wheel and dive and give a splendid display of aerobatics. Being so high, there is almost no sound of engines or cannon and the feeling of unreality is heightened.

59. EXT. ROHAN HOUSE: FRONT GARDEN. DAY
One of the German planes is hit. It trails smoke and goes into a dive. The spectators cheer or clap. DAWN thrusts her head out of an upper-floor window.

DAWN: What's all the shouting about?

BILL: We got one. An ME 109.

> (*There is a corporate gasp as the PILOT leaps from his burning plane and a parachute blossoms and checks his fall. GRACE draws the children back into the cover of the house as the plane crashes. They creep out again. The dog fight continues but the German planes have lost formation and dispersed. The battle has become straggly and is rapidly disappearing from view. Meanwhile, the PILOT's parachute drifts ever closer as he descends, causing great excitement.*)

60. EXT. ROSEHILL AVENUE. DAY
Neighbours run in the direction of the falling airman. Some women

carry garden forks and others pick up rocks on the way. GRACE *and the children hurry back into the house.*

61. EXT. ROHAN HOUSE: GARDEN. DAY
They go out through the back gate to join an excited throng of neighbours.

62. EXT. BUILDING SITE. DAY
The PILOT *drifts down on to the wasteland where the barrage balloon bravely flies. People rush in from all sides, as he makes an elegant landing and gathers his parachute. A crowd of women, children and old men encircle him, but keep a respectable distance. He surveys them coolly. He looks no more than twenty years old. The crowd watches every move he makes. They edge back as he reaches into his pocket. But it is only a silk handkerchief that he pulls out. He wipes his hands, puts it away. He moves to an empty oil drum and sits on it. He crosses his legs and carefully lights a cigarette. He affects the greatest nonchalance as he smokes. A little way off a huge hoarding gives an artist's impression of the houses that were to be built on this site, an idyll of suburban bliss. The* PILOT *looks at the idealized family group on the poster and then at* GRACE *and her children. He smiles ironically.*

GRACE: England is so beautiful, and he had to land here of all places.
(*Finally, a rather aged* POLICE CONSTABLE *arrives on the scene. The onlookers thrust him forward. He advances a few paces, then stops, hesitating, quite at a loss. He looks at the* PILOT *then back to the crowd. They egg him on. Resolutely, the* CONSTABLE *pulls out his truncheon and steps forward.*)
CONSTABLE: Now then. Now then.
(*The German* PILOT *gets languidly to his feet. The* POLICEMAN *retreats a pace. A titter or two ripples through the crowd. Encouragingly, the* PILOT *half raises his hands in the 'stick-em-up' position, the cigarette held delicately between the pale fingers. It is a taunting but oddly gentle gesture. The* CONSTABLE *takes him by the arm and leads him off. The crowd opens up to let them pass. As he goes,* DAWN *catches his eye and he winks at her. She gives him a flirtatious smile.* GRACE *is horrified. She seizes* DAWN *and forces her face against her own breast, hiding her gaze from the lewdness of the enemy.*)

63. INT. ROHAN HOUSE: DAWN'S BEDROOM. NIGHT
DAWN *is bent over, looking between her legs at* BILL *as he tries to draw a stocking seam up the back of her calf. He must continuously lick the brown crayon. She holds a hand mirror in such a way that she can see the progress of his work.*
DAWN: It's crooked. Rub that bit out and do it again.
(*She cuffs him and he resumes. He stops halfway up her thigh.*)
Well, keep going. Don't stop now.
(*He goes higher, then hesitates again.*)
BILL: Nobody is going to see this far up.
(*She leers at him.*)
DAWN: Don't be so sure.
(*He blushes. She stands up and pirouettes, her flared skirt swings out, exposing her knickers.*)
When I jitterbug.

64. INT. DANCE HALL. NIGHT
DAWN, *skirt swinging as she jitterbugs with a young Canadian*

soldier, BRUCE. *They are good. He hoists her over his shoulder.*
They whirl and swirl. The music changes to a slow waltz.

BRUCE: It was great for me, how was it for you?

DAWN: A bit too quick.

BRUCE: Well, now we can do it slow. Are those some new kind
    of stockings you're wearing?

DAWN: They might be.

BRUCE: I mean, no suspenders. They just kinda disappear up
    your ass.

    (She slaps his face. He holds up his hands in mock horror and
    backs away.)

    Quit it. Help me, someone. This girl's beating on me.

    (Jeers and laughter from fellow Canadians on the dance floor.
    DAWN *turns and walks off, head in the air, but not forgetting to*
    wiggle her bottom as she goes. BRUCE *grins admiringly and*
    stalks after her on tiptoe. His pals love it.)

65. EXT. SKY. DAY
Black and white.

A Spitfire is attacked by a German plane. The pilot twists and turns, trying to escape. The pilot is BILL*! His eyes bulge with fear as the enemy bullets rip into his fuselage. The rat-a-tat of the gunfire wakes him up.*

66. INT. ROHAN HOUSE: CHILDREN'S BEDROOM. NIGHT
Colour.

BILL *opens his eyes, and they alight upon his model Spitfire suspended on a thread over his bed. The cannon fire gradually resolves into a tapping on his window. Blearily he gets up and unlatches it. A dishevelled* DAWN *climbs through, threading her way between the model airplanes hanging from the ceiling and stepping down over the table on which* BILL *has his shrapnel collection spread.*

BILL: (*Whispering*) Mind my shrapnel.

(DAWN *thrusts a brass regimental hat badge in* BILL*'s face.*)

DAWN: (*Whispering*) I'm starting my own collection.

BILL: (*Impressed*) It's Canadian. Where'd you get it?

(*She pockets it and creeps out of the door, smiling smugly.*)

67. INT. ROHAN HOUSE: DAWN'S BEDROOM. NIGHT
DAWN *pulls back the covers and slides into bed, fully dressed. She is asleep as her head hits the pillow. A distant siren starts up, warning of an air-raid.*

68. INT. ROHAN HOUSE. GRACE'S BEDROOM. NIGHT
GRACE *is instantly alert as the sirens call one to another, coming closer. She throws on her dressing-gown, pulls on her fur-lined boots, picks up the ever-packed bag at her bedside and hurries out of the door.*

69. INT. ROHAN HOUSE: CHILDREN'S BEDROOM. NIGHT
GRACE *shakes* BILL *and* SUE *awake.*
GRACE: Bill, Sue. Air-raid!
(*They tumble out of bed and into their dressing-gowns like automata.*)

70. INT. ROHAN HOUSE: DAWN'S BEDROOM. NIGHT
GRACE *enters, shakes* DAWN *who does not respond.* GRACE *pulls back the covers and is surprised to see* DAWN *fully dressed, wearing make-up and with slightly crooked seams down the back of her legs.*
GRACE: Dawn, what have you been up to?
(DAWN *murmurs her protest.* GRACE *pulls her out of bed, but* DAWN *crawls back in.*)
DAWN: I'm not going to that shelter. I'd sooner die.

71. INT. ROHAN HOUSE. STAIRS. NIGHT
Bombs are already falling. GRACE *switches on a light and hurries down the stairs leading her two children through the familiar routine. She calls back.* BILL *bumps down the stairs, on his bottom, half asleep.*
GRACE: Dawn! Come down here!
(*She starts back up the stairs, but is halted by a bomb dropping close by. She runs down again, scoops up the two little ones and heads for the living room.*)

72. INT. ROHAN HOUSE: LIVING ROOM. NIGHT
As they approach the french windows, another bomb explodes very close by. Before its sound is heard, there is a tremendous blast, which

67

rips off the blackout curtains and sends them floating into the room. The windows are torn out, and most of the fragmented glass hangs limply from the brown paper that criss-crosses the panes for just this eventuality. Every loose object is hurled inwards. The room light flickers on and off and shell-bursts illuminate the room from without. GRACE *and the children are thrown back against the wall, but before they hit it the process is reversed and the blast is sucked out again. They are pulled back towards the windows together with the glass and loose fragments of the room. This all happens slowly as though the room were filled with water and the windows were a reversible sluice gate.* SUE's *long blonde hair is first blown, then sucked across her face. Then comes the sound of the explosion itself, which seems to have the effect of draining the water from the room. The people and the bric-à-brac all drop to the floor, dead weights once more.*

The children clutch their ears, screaming. GRACE *has one or two cuts. She gathers up the children, spreading her blood on them, and frightens herself, confused as to whom the blood belongs. She wipes it away, crying out a desperate prayer.*

GRACE: Please, God. Take me, but spare them.
(*She carries* SUE *and drags* BILL *through the shattered french windows, out into the garden and towards the Anderson shelter.*)

73. EXT. ROHAN HOUSE: GARDEN. NIGHT
Two more bombs explode, further away, but still close enough for the blast to force them off balance. They stumble and fall, covering their ears against the pressure. They tumble into the shelter, stepping into several inches of water. The ack-ack keeps up a barrage, and the exploding shells intermittently light up the sky. GRACE, *mumbling Dawn's name, clambers out of the shelter to fetch her.*

GRACE *sees* DAWN *coming down the garden. She looks dazed as she staggers quite slowly with one arm wound around her head. As she gets closer,* GRACE *sees that her eyes are glazed and she is moaning.* GRACE *leads her into the shelter and covers her with a blanket.* SUE *is fast asleep already in spite of everything.* DAWN *looks at her mother accusingly.*

DAWN: You don't care if I die. How could you leave me there?

69

Even if you don't love me.
(DAWN *desperately wants her mother to take her in her arms,
but* GRACE *sits stiffly upright, unyielding.*)
Tell me the truth. You had to get married, didn't you?
Because of me.

GRACE: The ideas you get in your head.

DAWN: That's why you never liked me. I'm different from you.
Well, everything's different now, so it doesn't matter. So
there.

(*Finally* DAWN *bends forward and puts her head on her
mother's lap and cries, at first softly, then more bitterly.* GRACE
holds her and rocks her at last. BILL *watches this, perplexed, as
perhaps he always will be, by the complex emotional interplay
that passes between women.*)

74. INT. ROHAN HOUSE: LIVING ROOM. DAY
GRACE *and* DAWN *are clearing up the debris. Some plaster has
fallen and there is a pall of dust. They are singing merrily, glad to be
alive, to have survived the night.*

Outside the front window, BILL *and* SUE *can be seen, having
ventured out, eager to explore the damage done to Rosehill Avenue.*

75. EXT. ROSEHILL AVENUE. DAY
BILL *picks up shrapnel. Several houses have been damaged, one
heavily so. Outside this house, a handful of people has gathered
watching the ARP men as they comb through the smouldering ruins.
Two of them are working a stirrup pump as they extinguish a small
fire in a corner of a room. Some children come up to* BILL *and* SUE.
They are flushed and excited, bursting with news. One boy, ROGER,
blurts it out.

ROGER: Pauline's mum got killed.

BILL: No, she didn't.

ROGER: Yes, she did, didn't she?
(*He appeals to his companions, particularly to a girl,* JANE, *a
little older than the others.*)

JANE: Yes, she did. Killed stone dead.

ROGER: You can ask her. Ask Pauline.
(*He points over at the ruined house, and sure enough there is
*PAULINE, *a girl of twelve. From time to time, a solicitous*

70

neighbour goes over to her, offering help, but PAULINE *shakes her head and looks away. She just stands there as though her mother had told her to wait on that spot and not talk to any strangers until she got back. The children drift across towards her and stop a few feet away. They stare intently, studying her face.*)
Isn't that right? Your mum got killed last night.
(PAULINE *nods affirmatively. A boy throws a miniature parachute into the air. It opens up and drops neatly at* PAULINE'*s feet.*)
There you are. I told you.
(*He jabs* BILL *in the ribs, finding a physical vent for his excitement.* BILL *lashes back at him with a violent anger that scares and quells the other boy. The group falls silent.*
PAULINE *steals glances at them out of the corner of her eye. She is not a popular girl, careful and self-conscious, and she cannot help enjoying this situation. She flushes.*)
JANE: Do you feel rotten, Pauline?
(PAULINE *shakes her head. The children move away from her and start to fool around, scrapping and laughing, but when they get back within a certain distance of* PAULINE, *they grow quiet and move away again.* BILL *nudges* SUE.)
BILL: Go and ask her if she wants to play.
SUE: Ask her yourself.
BILL: You do it. You're a girl.
(SUE *edges slowly towards her, not without nervous glances back at her brother.*)
SUE: Pauline.
(PAULINE *does not deign to answer the little girl.*)
Pauline. Do you want some shrapnel?
(*She has some fragments in her hand. She offers them to* PAULINE. *It is possibly part of the bomb that killed her mother.* PAULINE *shakes her head.*)
Do you want to play?
(PAULINE *shakes her head again.* SUE *goes back to* BILL *who has been watching carefully at a distance. After a moment, they turn back and walk home.* ROGER *sees another newcomer approaching. He calls out.*)

ROGER: Hey, Terry. Pauline's mum got killed last night.
TERRY: She never.
ROGER: She did too.

76. INT. ROHAN HOUSE: LIVING ROOM. DAY
BILL *and* SUE *enter, bursting with their news.* GRACE's *sister,*
HOPE, *has come to help and so have* MOLLY *and* MAC, *and a*
neighbour, MRS EVANS, *the one on whom* DAWN *wished a bomb.*
GRACE's *arm is bandaged.* MAC *is scoring panes of glass with a*
diamond cutter. He has a dollop of putty. BILL *is immediately*
distracted and cannot resist kneading the putty. DAWN *brings in a*
tray of tea. They are all in high spirits, almost festive. SUE *tugs at*
her mother's skirt.
SUE: Pauline's mummy got deaded.
        (GRACE's *attention is elsewhere. She does not hear.*)
MOLLY: You're lucky up here. The East End's been burning
        for three nights. Incendiaries.
        (DAWN *hands the neighbour her tea.*)
DAWN: Still not been hit, Mrs Evans?
MRS EVANS: Touch wood.
DAWN: You had a near miss the other night.
MRS EVANS: I hear they're dropping diseased rats on the bomb
        sites.
DAWN: (*Winking at* BILL) Bill found this tiny little parachute.
        So that's what it was for.
        (*They all slurp their tea and talk at once.* HOPE *is dusting the*
        piano.)
HOPE: Is the piano all right, Grace? It was knocked clean over.
        (GRACE *goes over to it and opens the lid, runs her fingers over*
        the keys.)
GRACE: It seems to have survived.
MAC: Play something, Grace.
MOLLY: We never used to sing much before the war, did we?
        Not in the daytime anyway.
        (DAWN *starts to sing 'Mareseatoats and Doeseatoats and*
        Littlelambseativy' and GRACE *picks it up on the piano.* DAWN
        dances around the room. There is something wild and
        abandoned about her.)

72

MRS EVANS: Dawn's come on fast.

MOLLY: That's the war for you. Quick, quick, quick.

MRS EVANS: Didn't I see you with a soldier, Dawn?

(*It is just a teasing guess. She roars with laughter.*)

DAWN: Just doing my bit for the war effort.

(GRACE *stops playing.*)

GRACE: I won't have this vulgar talk in my house.

DAWN: It's only a joke, Mummy. I'm fifteen. I'm still at school.
I want to be a nun when I grow up.

(MAC *goes over to* GRACE. *He picks up some sheet music from a
pile scattered on the floor. He selects a piece and props it on the
music stand.*)

MAC: Try a few bars of old Fred, Grace.

(GRACE *is softened by his tone. Their eyes meet for a moment.
She turns the stool back to the keyboard and plays Chopin,
particularly poignant since the fall of Warsaw. They listen with
teary eyes. 'Mareseatoats and Doeseatoats' and Chopin. It is
the spirit of the Blitz.*)

SUE: (*Whispering to* BILL) Tell them about Pauline's mum.

BILL: Not now. They wouldn't believe me.

77. STOCK FILM
Black and white.

*The Chopin continues over scenes of bomb-ruined London,
desolate and devastated.*

78. EXT. BOMBED SITE. EVENING
Colour.

*A surreal landscape: a flight of stairs leading nowhere, an exposed
bathroom; a house entirely destroyed but for one fragment of wall
jutting up, and on it still hangs a picture.* BILL *wanders among these
wonders, scavenging. A marauding gang of boys approaches. They
spread out and move up on* BILL *from all sides, trapping him.*
ROGER, *the boy who told of Pauline's mother's death, is among
them and appears to be the leader.*

ROGER: What are you doing here? This is our territory.

BILL: Looking for shrapnel.

A BOY: What you got?

(*Two of them grab* BILL *and wrench his fist open, extracting a*

piece of metal.)
Look, a detonator.
(*The others gather round, scrapping and shoving for a better
look.* BILL *makes a run for it, but they seize him and wrestle
him to the dusty ground.*)
ROGER: Take him to HQ, but blindfold him first.
(BILL'*s arms are twisted painfully behind his back and his eyes
are covered with a very dirty handkerchief. They take him to a
ruined house.*)

79. INT. RUINED HOUSE. EVENING
*The room has a brazier, table and chairs. They remove the blindfold
and he sees a wondrous sight, a collection of bullets, shells and bomb
fragments.* ROGER *slaps the shell proudly.*
ROGER: Unexploded.
(BILL *shrinks back.*)
BOY: You were spying.
BILL: I never was.
ROGER: Yes, you were. Make him talk.
(*They twist his arm. Several of the boys are smoking. One
takes a .303 rifle bullet and tightens it into an old vice fixed to
the table.* BILL *is fighting back the tears.* ROGER *leans over*
BILL.)
BILL: I know a secret.
ROGER: What's that?
BILL: The Germans are dropping men on the bomb sites.
ROGER: Who told you that?
(*They loosen their grip on his arm.*)
BILL: My uncle's in the War Office. He said, 'Don't go on the
bomb sites. Boys are going missing all the time.'
ROGER: They're not.
(BILL *has captured their attention. They release him.*)
BILL: If you find them, hiding, they cut your throat. They have
to, or they'd get found out.
(*The boys begin to get nervous, glancing about them. The* BOY
*on the vice aims a nail at the top of the bullet, brandishing a
hammer in the other hand.*)
BOY: I wish one would come through the door now.

(*He hammers the nail and the bullet explodes, embedding itself in the door. They jump out of their skins.*)

ROGER: You want to join our gang?

BILL: I don't mind.

ROGER: Do you know any swear words?

BILL: Yes.

ROGER: Say them.

(BILL *is stubbornly silent.*)

Well, go on. Say them. You can't join if you can't swear.

BILL: I only know one.

(*They laugh derisively.*)

ROGER: Well, say that one then.

(BILL *cannot get himself to say it, try as he will. They groan and jeer.* BILL *forces it out, the one that he heard on the bomb site.*)

BILL: Fuck!

(*They fall respectfully silent, exchange covert looks.*)

ROGER: That word is special. That word is only for something really important. Now, repeat after me . . . Bugger off.

BILL: Bugger off.

ROGER: Sod.

BILL: Sod.

ROGER: Bloody.

BILL: Bloody.

ROGER: Now put them together. Bugger off, you bloody sod.

BILL: Bugger off, you bloody sod.

ROGER: OK. You're in.

(*He gets up, leading them out of the room.*)

Let's smash things up.

(*They go into a newly bombed house and, armed with stout sticks and iron bars, indulge in an orgy of destruction.* ROGER *has an air-gun and specializes in picking off light-bulbs.* BILL *is tentative at first, but the violence is infectious. Pent-up aggression bursts forth and he is wilder and worse than the others.*)

80. EXT. BUILDER'S YARD. DAY

ROGER *leads the way, clambering over a damaged wall and*

dropping into an enclosed yard. The others tumble after him and
ROGER *raises a warning arm and addresses the gang solemnly.*
ROGER: This is top secret.

> (*He points to a corner where dozens of sign-posts, uprooted from
> crossroads, have been piled against each other, their arms
> spread out forlornly announcing the names of towns and their
> distances.*)
> They pulled them up from the crossroads, so when the
> Germans land they'll lose their way.

BILL: Won't they have maps?
ROGER: They'll have to go to a shop to buy a map, stupid. Then
> they'll give zemselves avay vis ze vay zay tork.

> (*One* BOY *starts to goose-step and sing.*)

BOY: (*Singing*) Ven der Führer says
> Ve iss der master race,
> Ve vart, vart, vart,
> Right in der Führer's face.

81. INT. ROHAN HOUSE: LANDING AND STAIRS. NIGHT
DAWN, *watched by* BILL, *tiptoes down the stairs. She opens the
front door as silently as possible. Vera Lynn dispenses sexy
sentimentality on the wireless ('Sincerely Yours').* GRACE *appears.*
DAWN *is caught in the act.*
GRACE: And where do you think you're going?
DAWN: Out.
GRACE: You go up to bed this minute and take off that lipstick.
DAWN: No, I won't.

> (GRACE *flies at her, enraged, and slaps her head and face.*)

GRACE: You wouldn't dare defy me if your father was here.

> (DAWN *covers her head with her arms until* GRACE *stops,
> exhausted.*)

DAWN: If you've finished, I'm going.

> (*She steps out of the door.* GRACE *grabs her, tearing her blouse,
> and swings her back inside. They wrestle wildly, both
> whimpering and moaning.* BILL *watches from above as the
> fight imperceptibly transforms and mother and daughter are
> finally hugging each other and crying.*)

76

I want him. I want him so much. I'll kill myself if I can't
have him.

GRACE: There, there, my baby.

(GRACE *lets go and turns back towards the living room where
Vera Lynn wails a lament.*)

Go if you want. What does it matter? We might all be dead
tomorrow.

(DAWN's *make-up is smudged, her clothes torn.*)

DAWN: I can't go like this.

(GRACE *turns back and takes* DAWN's *hand.*)

GRACE: You'd better bring him home, if you really love him.
Don't kill love. You'll regret it for the rest of your life.

DAWN: Who said anything about love?

(GRACE *looks at her in dismay, and* DAWN *glares back,
spiteful and defiant. Vera Lynn's voice, which has sung all
through this on the wireless, now swells up to an emotion-laden
finale.*)

82. EXT. BOMBED SITE. EVENING

*The gang's HQ is even further improved. They have put in some
expensive furniture. They have a wireless and a cocktail bar that
opens out to reveal a nest of mirrors reflecting the bottles within. The
gang fools around, in and out of the room, smoking and drinking
beer. A girl walks past, throwing them a flirtatious look. It is
PAULINE, the girl who lost her mother in an air-raid. They whistle
and shout at her.*

BOY I: Want to see our den?

BOY 2: We got a bed.

(*They laugh bawdily and she turns up her nose. One of the boys
starts to wrestle with her. She struggles and giggles. They pin
back her arms and try to kiss her. Her breasts push against her
blouse like little apples.* ROGER *whispers something in her ear.
She protests.*)

ROGER: Go on, Pauline. Be a sport.

PAULINE: No, I won't. There's too many of you.

ROGER: One at a time.

PAULINE: No, I won't.

ROGER: I'll give you something.

(*He gets a box, opens it and shows it to her. It is full of looted jewellery, brooches, necklaces, cheap bracelets.* PAULINE *is delighted. She pokes around and chooses a necklace, puts it on.*)

PAULINE: All right. Line up.

(*They form an orderly queue and* PAULINE *pulls up her skirt. She holds her knickers open by the elastic so that it is possible to look inside. The boys file past, each peering inside her knickers for a second or two.*)

BOY 2: I seen better.

(BILL *is on the end. As his turn approaches, his face is tense with apprehension.*)

PAULINE: It won't bite you.

(*They all laugh at his expense. He swings punches, flaying in all directions. One or two land. They hurt the recipients and they hit back.* ROGER *calls a halt.*)

ROGER: Pack it in. It's time to smash things up.

83. EXT. BOMBED SITE. EVENING
They drift out and fan across the ruins.

84. EXT. ANOTHER BOMBED SITE. EVENING
The gang loot and pillage, smashing as they go. Behind a piece of broken wall, BILL *discovers a soldier and a girl clasped together, the girl pressed against a door.* BILL *moves closer. The soldier fumbles with her clothing, but she is so wild with passion that his efforts are impeded.* BILL *registers the familiar gasps and cries that he is becoming accustomed to hearing from the injured, the dying and the coupling. The girl moves her head and her face becomes visible over the soldier's shoulder. It is* DAWN. *She sees* BILL *as he sees her. She mouths the words, 'Go away.' He starts to shake and cry. He moves away, then on an angry impulse picks up a stone and throws it. The soldier lets out a cry. He turns, revealing himself as* BRUCE.

BILL: (*Shouting*) Fuck!

(*Hearing the sacred cry, the gang come running. They see* BILL *hurling stones and quickly join in.* BRUCE *protests angrily and throws a couple of rocks himself, but he is overwhelmed. He protects* DAWN *from the onslaught and they flee.*)

78

ROGER: Teach him a lesson. Think they can come over here and take our women.

BOY 2: Wasn't that your sister, Rohan?

(BILL *shakes his head, denying her.*)

85. INT. ROHAN HOUSE: LIVING ROOM. NIGHT

GRACE *is cutting down a coat for* SUE; BILL *is reading a comic, the* Dandy; DAWN *is darning stockings. On the wireless is Tommy Handley and* Itma. *The doorbell sounds and* DAWN *catapults from her chair to greet the visitor. She returns with* BRUCE, *now evidently a welcome and regular guest. He is greeted enthusiastically.* BILL *throws friendly punches, one wild one catches him in the crotch. He takes it bravely. He distributes largesse, a tin of corned beef and a packet of tea for* GRACE, *chewing gum for* SUE, *a model barrage balloon for* BILL *and a pair of nylons for* DAWN.

BRUCE: You need suspenders for this kind.

(*She laughs, then holds the stockings against her skin in a transport of sensual delight.*)

DAWN: I'm going to cross my legs and make that rustling noise.

(*Finally and dramatically,* BRUCE *pulls out a package in a brown-paper bag. He gives it to* GRACE. *She opens it. It is a piece of beef steak.* GRACE *is overcome.*)

GRACE: Steak! I can't remember the last time . . .

BRUCE: (*Crooning ironically*) 'The last time I saw sirloin . . .'

(GRACE *holds the raw meat in her two hands and impulsively kisses it.*)

Take it easy. I know your husband's been away a long time, but . . .

DAWN: Don't be so cheeky, Bruce.

(*He holds up his hands in supplication.*)

BRUCE: Sorry, sorry. Too long in the barrack room.

(Itma *has ended and a programme has started up about the evacuation of Dunkirk. Its tone is quasi-religious – patriotic as it tells of the armada of little boats heroically snatching the remnants of the British Army out of the jaws of the Nazis. Churchill's voice booms out of the wireless.*)

CHURCHILL: (*Voice over*) If the British Empire lasts for a thousand years, men will say, this was her finest hour.

(BRUCE *has been horsing around with* BILL, *and all the time* DAWN *devours him with her eyes.*)

GRACE: Oh, do let's listen to this. I never tire of hearing it. It gives me goose pimples.

BRUCE: You haven't been taking your orange juice.

(The insolent sally gives DAWN *the excuse to jump on him and force him on to the sofa and into respectful silence. Stirring music punctuates the dramatic narration, which celebrates the bravery of the soldiers fighting their last-ditch stand.* BRUCE *giggles.*)

Don't sound like the Dunkirk I was at. I saw no fighting. We did a lot of running backwards, though. Then we got to the beach and we couldn't run no more. And Jerry just sat there and let us alone. If he'd come after us, boy! *(Shakes his head and laughs as though it would have been the funniest moment of the war.*) We were beat so bad, discipline was all to hell. We told the officers to go jump in the briny. There was no grub but we broke into the wine stores, and everybody got smashed. When the boats came, a lot of guys threw away their gear and filled their kitbags with loot. One buddy of mine burst into a jeweller's, his backpack was full of gold and silver. We had to wade out to the boats and he was so heavy he couldn't haul himself up. He slipped and sank like a stone.

(He laughs again. The broadcast comes to its moving climax.)

GRACE: How can you say such things? Can't you hear what happened?

BRUCE: I was there.

NARRATOR: *(Voice over)* God laid his hand upon the waters and they were still. The armada of little boats brought their precious cargo into safe havens. They lived to fight another day.

*(*BRUCE *leaps up and runs backwards around the room, giggling.*)

BRUCE: He who turns and runs away lives to fight another day.

(The inspiring, patriotic music, Elgar, wells up.)

GRACE: I don't care what you say. It filled our hearts that day. The little people stood up for once against the tyrant. Stood

80

up and said no.
(BRUCE *is impressed, despite himself.* DAWN *is quite affected too, by her mother's deep feeling.*)
That's how we put up with the bombing and the rationing, because of Dunkirk. Because of the spirit of Dunkirk, and because of that we shall never give in, never.
(*The Elgar continues into –*)

86. NEWSREEL
Black and white.
A shot of troops being ferried from the Dunkirk beaches by the little boats. An open fishing boat is packed with soldiers, mostly standing, while two men row. The soldiers begin to sway and 'la-la' to the Elgar soundtrack. They are serious and sombre, except for one, BRUCE, *who is grinning.*

87. INT. ROHAN HOUSE: CHILDREN'S BEDROOM. NIGHT
Colour.
Flash cut of BILL *in bed, smiling in his sleep.*

88. EXT. DUNKIRK. DAY
Back to BRUCE *singing and smiling.*

89. EXT. ROSEHILL AVENUE. DAY
CLIVE, *leather helmet and goggles iced up, rides up to the Rohan house on a Norton motorbike. The street is snow-covered and the road covered in brown slush.* BILL *and* SUE *run out to greet him. He dismounts painfully, his huge army greatcoat is also rimmed with frost. His face is so stiff with cold that he cannot crack a smile and presents an intimidating figure to the children, who draw up short. When he speaks, he can hardly form words. He beats his gauntlets together trying to get his circulation going. He staggers alarmingly from the stiffness as he walks, and cramp in one leg makes him hop up and down.*
CLIVE: On the bike for five hours. Only got a thirty-six-hour pass.
(*He holds out his arms to them. They cower back, then turn on their heels and scurry into the house, calling their mother.*

81

CLIVE *hops and staggers after them.* DAWN *appears and, after the initial surprise, laughs herself silly.*)

90. INT. ROHAN HOUSE: DINING ROOM. NIGHT
CLIVE *has changed into civvies and is soaking his feet in a bowl of hot water. Tea has been laid and the family is assembled. They watch* CLIVE *warily. They have learned to live without him and his reappearance has upset the new balance.*
CLIVE: Hand me my backpack, Bill.
  (BILL *hands it to him and* CLIVE *proudly pulls out an unlabelled can and plants it firmly in the centre of the table.*)
GRACE: And what's that?
CLIVE: Jam.
  (BILL *and* SUE *jump for joy.*)
BILL and SUE: (*Chanting*) Jam! Jam! Jam!
GRACE: Jam? What kind of jam? It's not like any jam I know.
CLIVE: German jam. It's German jam.
  (*The table falls deathly silent. They stare at the can as though it was a time bomb.*)
It's all right. It came from a German ship. It got sunk, and

this stuff washed ashore, crates of it. Jam. Our fellows
found it on the beach, by the rifle range.
(GRACE *picks it up gingerly, turns it, searches the blank silver-
grey metal for a sign, a clue, a portent.*)
GRACE: We don't know anything about it.
CLIVE: Well, it's off ration. We know that.
GRACE: How do we know they didn't plant it there? They know
we're mad on jam. They could poison half the country.
(CLIVE *surveys the suspicious hostile faces. Angrily, he seizes
the can and jabs it clumsily with the can opener.*)
Come away, children. I don't want you to stand too close
while he's opening it.
(*They retreat to the corner of the room.* CLIVE *has it opened and
bends back the top to reveal a deep-red jam.* GRACE *ventures
forward and peers at it.*)
CLIVE: Well?
GRACE: It looks . . . foreign.
CLIVE: Jam is jam! It's just jam!
DAWN: Well, I'm not having any. Even if it's not poisoned. I
don't think it's right. It's not patriotic.
BILL: You don't like jam. You hate jam. You never eat jam.
DAWN: That's not the point.
(*There is an impasse. They stare at it gloomily.* CLIVE *waves
grandly at the jam.*)
CLIVE: Taste it. Why don't you taste it?
GRACE: You taste it.
(*The eyes turn on* CLIVE. *The situation focuses their resentment
for one who has not shared their hardships, who abandoned
them, in fact. The jam has become a test. He looks into the
faces of his family. Resolutely, he takes up a teaspoon, picks up
the can and begins to eat. Grimly and steadily he ladles the jam
to his mouth. They watch him carefully for signs of pain.
Before their doubts are dispelled, he has consumed a third of the
can.* BILL *is the first to crack.*)
BILL: Give us some, Dad.
(CLIVE *stops eating, puts the can back on the table and they all
dig in. The tension is dispelled.* SUE *climbs on* CLIVE's *lap and
he feeds her himself. They laugh and chatter and stuff bread*

and jam into their mouths.)

GRACE: You mean they let you go through the officer training course and then said you were too old for a commission?

CLIVE: That's it.

GRACE: Why didn't they say before you started?

CLIVE: I wasn't too old when I started the course. I was too old when I finished it.

GRACE: What are you going to be then?

CLIVE: A clerk. I'm doing a typing course. I'll be typing for England.

(GRACE *goes to him, puts an arm around him.*)

GRACE: Poor Clive. You wanted it so much.

(*He looks up at her, beaten, uncomprehending. She kisses him.*) You're such a baby.

(*The doorbell sounds.* DAWN *scoots out to answer it.*)

BILL: It's lovely jam. It's nearly as nice as English jam.

(CLIVE *grins, quickly recovered from his bad moment.*)

CLIVE: You know what I always say? Jam is jam, the world over.

(DAWN *reappears with* BRUCE. CLIVE *darts a querying look at* GRACE. *He winces at the sight of his little girl looking up adoringly at a Canadian soldier.*)

DAWN: Bruce, this is my father. Dad, this is Corporal Bruce Carey.

(CLIVE *laughs awkwardly, outranked.*)

BILL: Bruce, look! Dad got some German jam.

SUE: We thought it was poison.

(*They laugh.* BRUCE *looks at it with mock suspicion, then tastes it with his fingertip. His eyes bulge and he clutches his throat.*)

BRUCE: The poison was at the bottom.

(*He falls to the ground in the most agonized convulsions. The children scream with laughter and jump on top of him.*)

91. EXT. ROHAN HOUSE: KITCHEN STEPS. DAY
The kitchen door is open, admitting thin winter sunlight. GRACE *works within. Outside,* CLIVE *is cleaning his kit, helped by* BILL. *Belt and gaiters are blancoed and laid out to dry.* CLIVE *is sitting on*

the steps, putting dubbin on his boots, BILL *polishing his father's hat badge, totally absorbed in its beauty.* GRACE *appears, puts a hand on* CLIVE's *shoulder, closes her eyes, lets the sun caress her face.*

GRACE: When do you think you'll get leave again?

CLIVE: Not till Christmas, I don't suppose.

(SUE *appears and sprawls herself across her father's lap.*)
I'm glad you didn't send them to your aunt.

GRACE: I had a letter from her. They've moved house.

CLIVE: Where to?

(*She smiles, eyes still closed.*)

GRACE: Woolamaloo.

(CLIVE *splutters with amusement.*)

CLIVE: Not Woolamaloo?

(BILL *looks up, grinning.*)

BILL: Woolamaloo? We would have lived in Woolamaloo?

(CLIVE *starts to sing the old music-hall song.*)

CLIVE: (*Singing*) W—O—O—L—A—M—A—L—O—O, oo.
Upon my word, it's true.
It's the way to spell
Woolamaloo.

(*They join in, in a ragged way, knowing it well.*)

EVERYBODY: (*Singing*) I bet you a dollar,
There isn't a scholar,
To spell it right first go, O,
W—O—O—L—A—M—A—L—O—O Loo—O

(DAWN *comes through the kitchen with* MAC *and* MOLLY, *who find the Rohans in high spirits. There are warm greetings all round.*)

92. EXT. ROSEHILL AVENUE. DAY

BILL *is giving his father and* MAC *a tour of the bomb damage. He picks his way expertly through the rubble, and they clamber after him.*

CLIVE: What kind of war is this, Mac? Up there in
Cumberland, we never see an air-raid. The worst problem I
have is getting a new typewriter ribbon. When I rode in
against the Turks, I knew what it was about.

MAC: Did you? You thought you did. We've been gypped, all

our lives. Look at your street.

(*They pause, looking out of a shattered window on to the street. It is a monotonous row of semi-detached houses, lying between other identical rows, now pocked with bomb damage, drab and drear.*)

CLIVE: What about it?

MAC: Rosehill Avenue. No roses. No hill. And it's certainly not an avenue.

CLIVE: Why not?

MAC: You need trees for an avenue.

CLIVE: There was talk of planting some when we first came.

MAC: Propaganda. We've been had.

(*They fall silent, watching* BILL *as he greets some other boys.*)

CLIVE: How's your war, Mac?

MAC: Never done better. On the fiddle. Like everyone else.

CLIVE: Except the servicemen.

MAC: Naturally.

CLIVE: I don't understand. Is there no point to any of it?

MAC: There is all right. This Hitler fellow. We've got to winkle him out. And get shot of some of our lot at the same time.

(*They watch* BILL *rooting about in the rubble.*)

CLIVE: Look how wild the boy's got. As for Dawn. Sixteen, going around with a soldier. (*Shakes his head.*) Keep an eye on them for me, Mac, there's a pal. I've made a mess of it all. (*His voice cracks. A sob wells up.*) I've been such a bloody fool.

(BILL *has come up behind them and watches covertly.* MAC *clasps* CLIVE *in his arms.*)

MAC: You always were, Clive. Steady the Buffs.

CLIVE: Bugger the Buffs.

(*Cries and shouts come from the street.* BILL *swings across a crater on a dangling electric cable and scrambles into the road. There is panic and pandemonium. The local barrage balloon's fins have punctured and it has lost stability. It is careering wildly like a kite out of control.* CLIVE *and* MAC *clamber into the street as the balloon skids across the sky, its steel cable shearing a chimney stack, which tumbles down into a front garden sending people scattering in all directions.* BILL *runs up,*

86

mad with excitement, as SUE *and* DAWN *come out of the house with* GRACE *and* MOLLY *and look up.* CLIVE *sprints across to them.*)

Take cover! We're being attacked by our own balloons!
(*They take no notice of his entreaty, curiosity getting the better of them.*)

MOLLY: It's having a nervous breakdown.
(*She giggles. The balloon bumps on the rooftop then shoots up into the sky again.* GRACE *starts to laugh.*)

GRACE: It's so wonderful.
(CLIVE *earnestly dashes back and forth, wanting to do something, but completely unable to decide what.*)

CLIVE: Don't panic! (*Goes over to* MAC.) Keep your head!

MAC: I will if you will.
(*The balloon does a fat little waltz in the sky.* CLIVE *suddenly explodes with laughter.* DAWN *has* SUE *in her arms.*)

DAWN: He just got fed up with all the other boring old barrage balloons and decided it was time to have some fun.
(*Two ARP men run down the street, urging people to go inside. The family retreat grudgingly towards their house, but hover in the front garden watching and laughing. Six Home Guards march into Rosehill Avenue at the double. The balloon has risen into the sky and the people are drawn out again into the street, looking up. The Home Guards come to a halt and raise their rifles.*)

BILL: Boo! Leave it alone!
(*The balloon suddenly plunges down towards the street, scattering the Home Guards. Women scream and everyone dashes for cover again.* BILL *laughs derisively.*)

They're scared of old fatty.
(*The Guards form up again and fire at the balloon. It bursts into flames. The shreds of burning cloth, followed by the spiralling cable, plunge into the street. There are cries of regret and the family and others step forward to inspect the smouldering remains with the same sadness that is felt at the end of a firework display.*)

Why did they have to go and do that?

93. INT. WVS CENTRE. DAY
*A make-do-and-mend session, where clothes are exchanged,
repaired, altered and cut down. It is swarming with women and
children.* MOLLY *and* GRACE *rummage among the racks of clothing.*
SUE *and* BILL, *bored and resigned, are obliged to try on items of
used clothing.*
MOLLY: God, how I hate all this scrimping and squalor.
GRACE: I don't mind it. It was harder before the war. Trying to
 keep up appearances. Now, it's patriotic to be poor.
 (*In the absence of men, women are everywhere stripping down
 to their underwear to try on clothes.* BILL *tries not to watch,
 acutely embarrassed.*)
MOLLY: I don't know how you cope, Grace. Three kids, Army
 pay. On your own.
GRACE: You know something, Molly? I like it on my own. I
 never got used to sharing a bed, not really.
 (MOLLY *pulls off her dress and suddenly, inches from* BILL's
 *face, are those mysterious few inches of white suspendered leg
 between the stocking-tops and the camiknickers.*

89

MOLLY: I love a man in bed, the smell of him, the hairiness rubbing against you, the weight of him. And when they do it to you in the middle of the night and you don't know if you're dreaming or it's really happening to you. That's the best. No guilty feelings. Not that I should have any, wide awake.

(MOLLY *pulls on a flowered silk dress that clings to her figure. She smooths it out.*)

GRACE: Molly!

MOLLY: Well, I'm not talking about Mac. He hasn't touched me for ages. And not often ever. My life started when Mac went on nights.

(*She dissolves in a fit of giggles.* GRACE *helps* SUE *with a sensible navy-blue coat. It is heavy and dull.* SUE *doesn't like it. Her face creases and tears well up.*)

GRACE: You're having me on, Molly.

MOLLY: Am I? Maybe I am.

GRACE: You've been drinking. You're tipsy.

MOLLY: Tipsy, topsy, turvy.

94. INT. ROHAN HOUSE: CHILDREN'S BEDROOM. NIGHT

BILL *and* SUE *each have a torch, which serve as searchlights.* BILL *smokes a Woodbine and he blows the smoke around his suspended model aircraft. Spitfires, Hurricanes, Messerschmitts, Heinkels are picked out in turn. As they appear,* BILL *simulates their engine noise. With considerable dexterity, he uses his free hand to fire his ack-ack guns, and papier-mâché pellets, pre-soaked in ink, fly through the air.* BILL *imitates a distressed plane plummeting to earth. His triumph is interrupted by a tap on the window. Expertly he dogs his Woodbine then goes to the window. He opens it and* DAWN *steps through. He is about to close it after her when* BRUCE'S *face appears.* BILL *lets fly an ink pellet catching* BRUCE *square on the forehead.* DAWN *holds up a threatening hand and the children shrink back as* BRUCE *clambers in. The two of them tiptoe into the next bedroom,* DAWN *throwing a warning glance over her shoulder.*

95. INT. ROHAN HOUSE: LANDING. NIGHT

BILL *and* SUE *share the keyhole, which affords a partial view of*

Dawn's bed. Complicated combinations of limbs cross the field of view, offering a tantalizing vision of events within. The children give up and return to their room, whispering.

SUE: I suppose they're still learning, that's why they keep moving about.

BILL: It's easy. I've done it.

SUE: Who with?

BILL: Pauline.

SUE: Liar. Mummy keeps still and Daddy moves on top of her. That's what they do when they know how.

96. INT. ROHAN HOUSE: DAWN'S ROOM. NIGHT
BRUCE *turns on his back with a deep sigh of satisfaction.*

BRUCE: (*Whispering*) Boy, that was some air-raid.

DAWN: Air-raid?

BRUCE: Didn't you feel the house rock? You must have seen all those shell-bursts.
(*She sticks the pillow in her mouth to stop laughing.* BRUCE *turns and whispers in her ear.*)
Let's get married. We'll live in Montreal. I'll teach you French. *Je t'aime, mon petit chou.*
(*Even when he is serious, his manner is teasing.*)

DAWN: Don't get smoochy. You'll spoil it.
(*She is genuinely irritated.*)

97. FILM EXTRACT
Black and white.

A scene from a forties romantic movie. The couple on the screen are deeply in love, but he must go off to the war. Their parting is bitter-sweet, prolonged and accompanied by a symphony orchestra playing its heart out.

98. INT. CINEMA. NIGHT
Colour.

MAC *sits between* MOLLY *and* GRACE. *He looks from one to the other. They are both weeping, lost in the movie, and oblivious of him.* SUE *sleeps, lying across her mother's lap.* BILL *squirms with embarrassment as the screen lovers kiss. He turns his face away. When he looks back, he is disgusted to see that they are still at it.*

99. EXT. NATIONAL GALLERY. DAY
BILL *leans over the balustrade of the pillared portico looking out on to Trafalgar Square. The strains of a passionate piano recital reverberate from inside the Gallery. Soldiers and their girls, hand in hand, listen enraptured.*

100. EXT. TRAFALGAR SQUARE. DAY
Barrage balloons hang over Admiralty Arch and garland Nelson astride his column.

101. EXT. NATIONAL GALLERY. DAY
BILL *threads his way through the crowd, past signs announcing Dame Myra Hess's lunchtime concerts (SOLD OUT) and into the marbled hall.*

102. INT. NATIONAL GALLERY. DAY
BILL *slides back into his seat next to* GRACE *as Dame Myra concludes the Warsaw Concerto. The audience rises to its feet, applauding.* GRACE, *her eyes shining, is among them.* MAC *watches her pleasure with pleasure.* BILL *is disturbed by the music, by the eruption of emotion all around him. There are many servicemen in the audience and some wearing the blue uniforms denoting the war wounded. They clap and clap.*
GRACE: Mac, that was wonderful. I haven't been to a concert since . . .
MAC: . . . since I used to take you to the Proms?
GRACE: That's right. Not since then. Not since I got married.
(*Their eyes meet. The audience is drowning in its own applause. Everyone is crying, or laughing, or both.* GRACE *and* MAC *among them. In the emotional tumult they reveal more than they intend. The audience falls silent.* BILL's *gaze drifts to the wall where huge paintings by official war artists hang.* GRACE *tears her eyes away from* MAC. *She senses* BILL *watching her and turns her attention to Dame Myra's fingers flying over the keys.*)

103. INT. ROHAN HOUSE: DINING ROOM. DAY
The table has been stretched to embrace the Rohan family, including

92

CLIVE, MAC *and* MOLLY, GRACE'S PARENTS, *and two of*
GRACE'S SISTERS. *They wear paper hats, have finished their*
Christmas dinner, and are listening attentively to King George VI
stuttering painfully through his Christmas message.

104. EXT. ROSEHILL AVENUE. DAY
It is raining. BRUCE *hurries along the street, and as he enters the*
Rohan's front gate, he pauses, pulls an old silk stocking over his
head and takes two glass eyes from his pocket. They look as though
they once belonged to a stuffed stag. He pushes them inside the
stocking and positions them just under his own eyes so that he can
peek over them. He crawls under the bow window.

105. INT. ROHAN HOUSE: DINING ROOM. DAY
The King falters to a conclusion.
CLIVE: He was a lot better this year.
    (MAC *and the others mumble agreement.*)
BILL: You said that last year, Dad.
CLIVE: The land and the King are one, my son. If he stutters,
    we falter. He's getting better, and so are we.

(The National Anthem strikes up on the wireless. They all rise and stand to attention.)

106. EXT. ROHAN HOUSE. DAY
BRUCE *raises his head and presses his grotesque face to the window. He taps on the glass. He is startled to see the assembled family standing upright and staring back at him without expression. He cavorts and waves his arms, but still gets no response. Sheepishly, he slinks into the porch and pulls off the stocking. The door opens to reveal* DAWN.
DAWN: Dad's furious. It was 'God Save The King'.
(He goes inside as she closes the door. He pushes the stag's eyes into his own sockets and scrunches up his face to grip them into place. DAWN *turns back and he lunges, trying to kiss her. She squeals with laughter.)*

107. INT. ROHAN HOUSE: DINING ROOM. DAY
A charade is in progress. CLIVE *and* MAC *are got up as prostitutes, wearing their wives' clothes.* GRACE *and* MOLLY *are dressed as men. There is a lot of salacious flirting and an argument breaks out over the price of whores.* MOLLY *says the word 'tart' emphatically and* BILL *jumps out of his seat, yelling.*
BILL: Jam tart! Jam tart! I got it! I got it!
(The four actors abandon their characterizations and applaud young BILL. BRUCE *watches in amazement.)*
BRUCE: Jesus Christ! This is Christmas?
*(*GRACE'S FATHER *rises, his glass held aloft.)*
GRANDFATHER GEORGE: Time for my annual toast. Charge your glasses.
(There are groans and mutterings of disapproval. He cuts an impressive figure, white hair, drooping moustache, waistcoat and watch-chain. His eyes take on a faraway look, sombre and serious. His wife pointedly leaves the room, slamming the door behind her.)
To Mary MacDonald, Thelma Richardson, Bobo Hinds, Lily Sanderson . . . *(Savours each name, smiles, shakes his head, has a special emphasis or tone of voice for every one of them.)* . . . Little Sarah Whatsit, now there was spirit. And Marjorie Anderson.

94

GRACE: Father, that's enough now.

GRANDFATHER GEORGE: And ... and ... Henry Chapman's girl, was it Thelma? No, I can see those cornflower eyes ... I've lost your name, my sweetness.

(*Tears come to his eyes. He falters. There are cries of 'shame'. HOPE, GRACE's sister, jumps to her feet.*)

HOPE: Do we have to listen to this nonsense every year? You're drunk, Dadda. Sit down.

GRANDFATHER GEORGE: ... Betty Browning ... Betty, let me tell you something. I'm seventy-three years old. I've seen half the wonders of the world and I never laid eyes on a finer sight than the curve of Betty Browning's breasts ... (*Raises his glass again*). My girls. Dead you may be, or old and withered. But while I live, I will do you honour to the last. Bless all of you.

(*He drinks and slumps down into his chair, overcome with melancholy. Only MOLLY applauds and only DAWN looks sympathetic. BILL taps his grandfather's knee.*)

BILL: It was Sheila, Grandpa.

(GRANDFATHER GEORGE *looks up sadly.*)

GRANDFATHER GEORGE: What's that?

BILL: Henry Chapman's daughter. It was Sheila. I remember her from last year.

(GRANDFATHER GEORGE's *face lights up. He ruffles* BILL's *hair.*)

GRANDFATHER GEORGE: So it was. Sheila. This boy will go far.

(BILL *turns away to* DAWN, *stifling his giggles.*)

BILL: I made it up!

108. EXT. ROHAN HOUSE. NIGHT

DAWN *and* BRUCE *kiss goodbye in the porch. She pulls away, sensing something amiss.*

DAWN: Something's wrong!

(*He looks away, unhappy and awkward.*)
What is it?

BRUCE: We're not supposed to say, but we're being shipped out tomorrow.

DAWN: Where?

BRUCE: I don't know.

DAWN: You do, you do. You're just not saying.

BRUCE: I swear I don't know. (*Offers her a little box.*) Here's
your Christmas present.

(*She opens it. A diamond ring. She gasps, then thrusts it back
at him angrily.*)

DAWN: You expect me to spend the rest of the war sitting at
home staring at a ring? And you'll meet some French girl
who can speak your own language. No thank you!

BRUCE: Please yourself.

(BRUCE *hurls the little box into the next-door bomb site and
storms off into the night.* DAWN *slams the door.*)

109. INT. ROHAN HOUSE: LIVING ROOM. NIGHT
DAWN *buries her head in a cushion, crying and wailing.* Only MAC *and* MOLLY *of the guests remain, and they are playing cards with* CLIVE *and* GRACE. GRACE *goes to comfort* DAWN.
GRACE: What is it, pet?
DAWN: He's being posted. I was horrible to him.
GRACE: Don't leave it like that. Go after him. Swallow your pride.

110. EXT. ARMY CAMP. DAY
CLIVE, *with* DAWN *riding pillion, pulls up at the Guard House on his old Norton.* DAWN *slides down and hurries to the Guard House.* CLIVE *props up the bike and follows her. A convoy of trucks pulls out of the gates. Soldiers lean out of the back of the lorries, cheering and whistling when they see* DAWN.

111. INT. GUARD HOUSE. DAY
The SERGEANT *of the Guard sits toasting his toes on a coke stove.* DAWN *addresses* CLIVE *as he enters.*
DAWN: We've missed them. They've gone. (*Turns back to the* SERGEANT.) Can't you tell me where? You can see I'm not a spy.
SERGEANT: I would if I could, but I can't.
(*He points to a wall on which two posters are pinned. One says, 'Careless Talk Costs Lives', the other 'Walls Have Ears'.* DAWN *is shattered.* CLIVE *puts an arm about her.*)
CLIVE: He'll write as soon as he can.
SERGEANT: Sure, he will. You'll meet again (*sings*) don't know where, don't know when. In the meantime, I am free tomorrow night.
(CLIVE *leads her out. A sprig of mistletoe hangs over the door.* DAWN *rips it down and flings it back at the* SERGEANT. *It hits him square in the face.*)

112. EXT. ROHAN HOUSE: PORCH. DAY
CLIVE *is packed up, ready to go. The family has come to bid farewell, all except* BILL, *who suddenly appears with a triumphant whoop.*

97

BILL: I found it! I found it!

(*He hands the little ring box to* DAWN. *She opens it and looks at the ring, but does not put it on her finger.* CLIVE *and* GRACE *watch tenderly.*)

DAWN: You needn't have bothered, Bill.

(*They watch* CLIVE *as he rides away. Behind them, the Christmas tree can still be seen in the window. As they turn to go in,* GRACE *looks warily at* DAWN.)

GRACE: That letter this morning, was it from Bruce?

(DAWN *nods.*)

What did he say?

DAWN: He said I was right. I shouldn't wait for him. It was better to make a clean break.

GRACE: I think it's very sensible in the circumstances.

DAWN: Now he's gone and made me fall in love with him, which I never wanted to do. I told him that.

(*She runs into the house and up the stairs.*)

113. EXT. SEASIDE RESORT. DAY

GRACE, MAC, BILL *and* SUE *are finishing a frugal picnic on the beach. They are muffled up against the nip of early spring. The sand is criss-crossed with pointed iron spikes and coils of barbed wire.*

98

Curt signs warn against mines and other hazards. BILL *and* SUE
*start to play happily and messily in the sand. In the distance, they
hear muffled, deep-throated explosions.*

BILL: What's that?

(MAC *gets up and scrutinizes the horizon.*)

MAC: Big Berthas, shelling France. Twenty-five-mile range,
they have.

BILL: Wow!

MAC: They send over a few every day, to let them know we're
still here. Each shell costs as much as a Ford 8.

BILL: Who pays for them?

MAC: We will, you will, for the rest of our lives.

(BILL *gets out a rubber ball, and spins it in his fingers.*)

GRACE: Remember this beach, Mac? All those summers. Our
two families, together.

MAC: Happy days. (*Watches* BILL's *efforts with the ball.*) When
you're a bit bigger, Bill, I'll teach you the googly.

(BILL *smiles a secret smile.*)

BILL: Thanks.

(GRACE *starts to sing.*)

GRACE: (*Singing*) There'll be blue birds over,
The white cliffs of Dover . . .

(MAC *and the children join in.* BILL *practises his spin, finger
and wrist.*)

ALL: (*Singing*) . . . tomorrow.
Just you wait and see . . .

(*Another 'crump' from Big Bertha.*)

BILL: There goes another Ford 8, Uncle Mac.

114. EXT. RAILWAY. NIGHT
*The train is unlit to comply with the blackout, the only illumination
being as the fire-box door of the loco is opened.*

115. INT. TRAIN COMPARTMENT. NIGHT
*Moonlight flickers intermittently into the compartment, lending a
jerky, monochromatic quality to the scene.* SUE *sleeps, thumb in
mouth.* BILL *dozes in the corner of the compartment.* GRACE *and*
MAC *sit side by side.*

GRACE: (*Softly*) Mac, did you ever find out who Molly went off with?

MAC: A Polish pilot. It's like one of those jokes on the wireless. (*He stares out of the window, the pale broken light making patterns on his face.*)

GRACE: You miss her. I know I do. (*He smiles ruefully.*)

MAC: She said, 'I know you love me, Mac, but you've never loved me enough.'

GRACE: Not loving enough. That is a terrible thing to do to someone. I suppose I did it to Clive. Always held something back. (*BILL stirs and fidgets, half hearing, squinting through drooping lids. MAC and GRACE lower their voices further, whispering.*)

MAC: It's all better left unsaid, Grace.

GRACE: You were never apart, you and Clive. He kept asking and asking. And I waited and waited for you to say something. And you never did.

MAC: Clive had a job. I didn't. I couldn't. (*They fall silent. GRACE smiles, ruefully.*)

GRACE: He could always make me laugh.

MAC: We did the decent thing.

GRACE: This war's put an end to decent things. I want to close my eyes and jump and give myself for once, hold nothing back.

MAC: We can't change what's past. Not even the war can do that.

GRACE: We did all the proper things, and we lost love. That's sad, Mac. (*Their eyes meet and acknowledge what might have been, of happiness accidentally missed.*) If I saw this at the pictures, I'd be crying my eyes out, but I can't shed a tear for myself. (*In the pale half-light, they seem young and innocent. He takes her hand. They almost kiss. But for the children, they would. Finally, MAC turns away and looks at the dark, heavy shapes of the approaching city.*)

116. EXT. ROSEHILL AVENUE. NIGHT
As GRACE, MAC, BILL *and* SUE *turn into the avenue, they see a house burning. It is theirs. When they get closer, they see it is gutted and the roof has collapsed. The firemen have hoses trained on it, but it is too hot to get into the front door.* GRACE's *first thought is for her daughter.*
GRACE: Dawn! Dawn!
(DAWN *is with a knot of neighbours, watching the blaze.* GRACE *is so relieved to see her that she smiles and becomes quite tranquil.*)
Thank God you're safe.
(*The* FIRE CHIEF *approaches her.*)
FIRE CHIEF: Was this your house, madam?
GRACE: I didn't know there was a raid.
FIRE CHIEF: It wasn't a bomb, just a fire.
GRACE: What do you mean, a fire?
FIRE CHIEF: It happens in wartime as well, you know.
(MAC *is shattered. He puts an arm round* GRACE. *She throws him a look, haunted with guilt, and she moves away to console her children, who watch the blaze impassively.*)
DAWN: I just wish I'd worn my nylons.
(GRACE *is suddenly seized by a dread thought. She runs to the* FIRE CHIEF.)
GRACE: My ration books are in there!
(*She makes a wild dash at the house, but* MAC *and neighbours restrain her.* BILL *remains next to the* FIRE CHIEF.)
BILL: My shrapnel collection should be all right.
FIRE CHIEF: Oh yes, I should think so.

117. EXT. ROHAN HOUSE. DAY
Mac's car drives up to the charred ruins of the house. GRACE *and the children get out.* ROGER *and his gang are already out looting.* BILL *charges* ROGER *and punches him in the face. They fall and roll in the wet ashes. The bigger boy is so taken aback by* BILL's *ferocity that he cannot gain an advantage.* MAC *stops* GRACE *from interfering, understanding the boy's need.* PAULINE *has appeared and smiles knowingly as she watches. Other children gather.* ROGER *picks himself up and the gang beats a retreat.*

101

118. INT. ROHAN HOUSE. DAY

GRACE, MAC, DAWN *and* SUE *join* BILL *in the house and scratch among the debris to see what can be salvaged.*

119. EXT. ROSEHILL AVENUE. DAY

They ferry bits and pieces back to the car. GRACE *discovers the charred remnants of a photo album. There are pictures with unburnt fragments and she carries it carefully to the car.*

GRACE: Mac, look! Some of the snaps are saved.

(*It is open at a picture of the two families at the very beach they visited yesterday. It is burned around the edges, only* MOLLY *and* CLIVE *are unscathed and they smile happily.* GRACE *and* MAC *look at it and then each other. It feeds their guilt. The neighbours gather and awkwardly try to express their sympathy.* MRS EVANS *arrives with some clothes.*)

MRS EVANS: This coat should fit you, Grace. And here are some things for Dawn. And a few bits for the kitchen.

GRACE: Thank you, Evelyn.

(BILL *is acutely embarrassed. He catches* PAULINE'*s smirking look. He fights to hold back the tears, but finally fails.*)

It's only a house. We still have each other.

BILL: I don't care about the house, I just hate all these people watching us and being nice.

120. EXT. THE THAMES RIVERSIDE. DAY

Carrying GRACE *and the three children,* MAC'*s car draws up on the towpath facing an island on which is a number of wooden bungalows with verandas decorated in fretted scroll work. Neat lawns slope down to the river's edge where varnished punts and skiffs lie sleekly tethered.* GRANDFATHER GEORGE *has spotted them and he rear-sculls his dinghy across the water to fetch them.*

GRANDFATHER GEORGE: Coming. Coming. Deliverance is at hand. All will be well.

(GRANDMOTHER *comes down from the bungalow to the edge of the river and waves encouragingly.* BILL *is captivated by the river. Moorhens thread through the tendrils of a weeping willow. An electric slip launch is moored where they wait. He strokes its glassy varnish.* MAC *unloads the boot of the car.*)

MAC: Another world, eh, Bill? And not twenty miles from Piccadilly.

(GRACE *comes alongside* DAWN *and waves to her mother on the far bank, only forty yards away.* DAWN *glances nervously at* GRACE.)

DAWN: Are you strong enough for another shock? You're going to be a grandma. (*Waves across the river at her own* GRANDMOTHER.) Hello, Grandma.

(GRANDFATHER GEORGE *docks his craft expertly and lassoes a mooring post.* GRACE *lets out an hysterical cry.*)

GRACE: I don't believe this is happening to me.

DAWN: It's not. It's happening to me.

GRANDFATHER GEORGE: (*Responding to* GRACE) It's only a house, and a ghastly one at that. They should all be burned and bombed and the builder hanged.

(MAC *and* GRANDFATHER GEORGE *load the family's few possessions on to the boat.*)

GRACE: What did I do to deserve this?

GRANDFATHER GEORGE: You married that fool, Clive, that's what. Never mind, you can stay with us.

GRACE: (*To* DAWN) How long?

DAWN: Three and a half months.

GRANDFATHER GEORGE: As long as that? Well, all right. Why not? It's nearly summer. Let the nippers run wild.

(*The children have got into the boat.* GRACE *turns to* MAC *and kisses him awkwardly.*)

GRACE: Bless you, Mac. What would I have done without you?

MAC: (*Ruefully*) You might still have a house.

GRACE: (*Wistfully*) I wish it could all have been different.

MAC: Look after yourself, Grace.

(*He watches them as they cross the river, conscious of the gap widening between himself and* GRACE.)

GRACE: Everything I have left in the world is in this little boat.

(BILL *studies* GRANDFATHER GEORGE's *sculling technique.*)

BILL: Can I try?

GRANDFATHER GEORGE: Put your hand on mine, get the knack of it.

(BILL *holds the gnarled old hand and moves in unison.*)

104

I shall teach you the ways of the river. Another year in that awful suburb and you would be past saving. Look, they're coming this way! The future on the march. I curse you, Volt, Watt and Amp.
(*Looming over* GRANDFATHER GEORGE's *bungalow is a newly constructed electric pylon.*)

121. INT. BUNGALOW: BILL'S AND DAWN'S BEDROOM. DAWN
BILL *wakes, looks out at the river.*

122. EXT. BUNGALOW. DAWN

A grey dawn light touches the mist lying over a glassy river. BILL *comes out of the house and stands at the edge of the water: not a breath of wind, not a soul stirring. He slips out of his grandfather's voluminous pyjama pants. Delicately, he lowers himself into the river, careful not to crack the perfect smoothness of the water. He slides slowly in until only his head is showing. He swims out into the centre of the stream, without disturbing the water. He stops, takes a breath, then submerges, leaving not a ripple, never a trace. The dawn river is once more unobserved, its secret self again.*

123. INT. BUNGALOW: BILL'S AND DAWN'S BEDROOM. DAWN

BILL *comes in wet from bathing, to find* DAWN *half dressed contemplating her slightly swollen navel. They share a small room in which are two bunk beds.*

DAWN: Have a listen. See if you can hear anything.
    (*With some reluctance,* BILL *puts an ear to her stomach. His cold wet hair gives her a shock. She slaps him.*)
    You're icy cold. A shock like that could give me a miscarriage. (*Grinning*) That's an idea, do it again.
    (DAWN *giggles and it is* BILL'*s turn to be shocked.*)
GRANDMA: (*Out of shot*) Breakfast, all!
    (DAWN *leaves the room while* BILL *climbs into his clothes.*)

124. INT. BUNGALOW: DINING ROOM. DAY

The room lets out, through open french windows, on to a back garden sown with vegetables for some yards and then giving way to orchard and pasture. The morning sun streams in. GRANDFATHER GEORGE *sits at one end facing the garden.* GRACE, SUE, GRANDMA *and* DAWN *flank him.* GRANDFATHER GEORGE *is not at his best in the morning. He glares at* BILL *as he enters and slips quietly into his seat.*

GRANDMA: Did they say how long it would take to get new ration books, Grace?
GRACE: (*Shouting and enunciating*) Up to six weeks, I think.
GRANDMA: How are we going to cope?
GRANDFATHER GEORGE: Nettle soup, like we did in the Great

War. Very nourishing. Bill and I will catch fish. The river
fowl will be laying eggs soon. We'll hunt. We'll forage.
We'll overcome.
GRANDMA: What about tea and sugar, clever Dick?
(GRANDFATHER GEORGE *holds up a warning hand.*)
GRANDFATHER GEORGE: Keep still! Nobody move!
(*His aspect fills them with dread. His eyes are boring holes in
the cabbage patch, outside the french windows, where a rat is
crouching.*)
(*Dramatic whisper*) Mother! Fetch my gun.
GRANDMA: What's that, dear?
(*He points urgently at where the gun stands against the wall.*
GRANDMA *creeps on tiptoe over to the gun and hands it to him,
resuming her place without making a sound. He raises the
shotgun, aiming along the length of the table. The children are
statues, only their eyes darting from him to the rat and back.
The barrel is inches from their faces. He fires. They jump.
Smoke fills the room. He curses under his breath, as the rat
escapes. He puts down the gun and readdresses his boiled egg.
As an afterthought, he turns to* BILL.)
GRANDFATHER GEORGE: Never let a rat creep up on you.
BILL: I think you hit him, Grandpa. He was limping when he
ran off.
(GRANDFATHER GEORGE *gives him a searching look, but
BILL is all innocence.* DAWN *stifles the giggles.* GRACE *sees
what goes on and suppresses a smile herself.* BILL *suddenly
coughs and splutters to hide his laughter.* DAWN *goes red in the
face, tears come to her eyes and her shoulders shake.* SUE
*suddenly tinkles with innocent mirth and the suppressed
laughter bursts out of them all. They roar and gasp and shudder
and cannot stop.* GRANDMA, *quite perplexed, smiles, happy to
see them all so happy.* GRANDFATHER GEORGE, *eyes blazing
with anger, glares at them disdainfully, but the dam has burst
and, fear him as they do, the laughter pours out unabated and
their eyes are filled with tears.*)

125. EXT. RIVER. DAY
GRANDFATHER GEORGE *poles the punt up river.* GRACE,

GRANDMA *and* SUE *lounge in the cushions.* BILL *stands alongside the old man, learning the way of it.*

GRANDFATHER GEORGE: Up, two, three. Throw the pole forward. Let it slide through your fingers. Don't push until it hits the bottom.

(BILL *takes it all in.*)

Now check that spinner.

(BILL *crawls along the shiny rear deck and hauls in a fishing line.*)

BILL: No luck, Grandpa.

(*He lets it out again. A wood-fired steam launch, all polished brass, with an elegant canopy, chugs past them. An elderly couple occupies it, seated in wicker armchairs.*

GRANDFATHER GEORGE *raises his cap to them.*)

GRANDFATHER GEORGE: Good day, ma'am. Greetings, Edward.

(*They are beguiled by the spell of the afternoon.* GRACE *trails her fingers dreamily in the water. Willows, bullrushes, glide past.*)

GRANDMA: . . . such nice boys with straw boaters and blazers. All the punts lit up with Chinese lanterns. Like fireflies. And the gramophone going on one of the boats. Always the Charleston, the Charleston, the Charleston. Oh, you girls.

GRACE: Wasn't it lovely?

(GRANDFATHER GEORGE *entrusts the pole to* BILL. *He struggles with the technique, does quite well. Then the pole sticks in deep mud. He cannot extricate it.*)

GRANDFATHER GEORGE: Let it go. Let it go.

(*But* BILL *hangs on to the pole and the punt moves on until he is stretched between them. Finally, he hops on to the pole and clings to it.*)

Stay put. Hang on.

(*He takes a paddle and drives the boat back to where* BILL *is stranded. The pole starts to topple in a slow arc.*

GRANDFATHER GEORGE *renews his efforts and* BILL *is able to step neatly on to the rear decking. The old man eases the pole from the mud.*)

Now there's a lesson for life. Never give up the punt for the pole.

108

126. EXT. GRANDFATHER GEORGE'S RIVERSIDE GARDEN.
DAY

Tea is being laid on the lawn by GRANDMA, GRACE *and* DAWN; GRANDFATHER GEORGE *reclines in the faded swing-seat.* BILL *ferries* FAITH, HOPE *and* CHARITY *(his three aunts) to the island in the dinghy. He rear-sculls with some difficulty, but well enough.* GRANDFATHER GEORGE *examines his daughters with binoculars as they 'ooh' and 'aah' greetings on their approach. They disembark and there is much hugging and kissing. They have all brought clothing for the family and dresses and blouses are held up, examined, admired.*

The daughters clearly disapprove of GRANDFATHER GEORGE *and offer only perfunctory kisses,* HOPE *ignoring him completely.* SUE *is held up and passed from hand to hand as though she were a frock herself. They take it in turns to shout clarification to their mother. They flutter around* DAWN, *who is now showing her pregnancy.*

FAITH: No word from Bruce, my pet?

(*It was meant well, but it makes* DAWN *bristle.*)
All men are beasts, darling.

DAWN: That's what I like about them.

FAITH: Dawn! Really!

(BILL *slides over to his grandfather.*)

GRANDFATHER GEORGE: All hens and no cocks. Too many
women in the family. They're a different species from us,
Bill. Love them, but don't try to understand them. That
road leads to ruin. Let's make a nuisance of ourselves.
(*He mingles among the women, deciding to goad his daughter*
HOPE.)
You look frustrated, Hopey. That husband of yours still
can't rise to the occasion?
(HOPE *flares up, but bites her tongue and turns away.*
GRANDFATHER GEORGE *turns to* BILL, *confidingly.*)
I won't have the husbands here. All four married duds
including your mother.

HOPE: He's a menace. He ought to be locked up.

CHARITY: Don't let him get his claws into Billy, Grace.

(GRANDFATHER GEORGE *continues his advice to* BILL.)

GRANDFATHER GEORGE: They'll tame you if they can, cage
you and feed you tidbits. Better retreat to prepared
positions.
(*He leads* BILL *round to the back garden away from the river.*
All the bungalows are built up on piers against flooding. He
reaches under the house and retrieves an old cricket bat and
ball. He throws the ball at BILL.)
Bags I bat first.
(*He takes guard against the trunk of an old apple tree.* BILL
twists his fingers around the ball and bowls a spinner to
GRANDFATHER GEORGE *who waits for it to break, then plays*
it back. The next ball breaks the other way and clean bowls
him. GRANDFATHER GEORGE *looks back at* BILL *with*
astonishment.)
That was a googly!

BILL: I know.

GRANDFATHER GEORGE: You're a dark horse, bowling
googlies at your age. Toss me up another.

BILL: No, you're out, Grandpa. It's my turn.

(*With ill grace,* GRANDFATHER GEORGE *surrenders the bat and offers a harmless arthritic delivery which* BILL *thumps into the gooseberry bushes.* GRANDFATHER GEORGE *curses and pricks his fingers as he tries to retrieve the ball. He looks up irritably at the sounds of laughter from his daughters. He snarls in their direction.*)

GRANDFATHER GEORGE: Want to know why they're called Faith, Hope, Grace and Charity?

BILL: Why?

GRANDFATHER GEORGE: Your grandmother. She named them after the virtues I lack. That's marriage for you.

(*He bowls again.* BILL *hammers it away.* GRANDFATHER GEORGE *glares at him, trembling with fury.*)

BILL: It's only a game, Grandpa.

(GRANDFATHER GEORGE *gets himself under control and trots off to find the ball.*)

127. EXT. RIVER. DAY

BILL *and* SUE *are in the dinghy, pushing into a stand of reeds.* BILL *hangs over the bows, hauling the boat along by pulling on the reeds. The parting rushes reveal a moorhen's nest, neatly suspended above the water on bent-over reeds meshed together. There are some dozen speckled eggs.* BILL *carefully extracts one of them and places it in a little basket in the boat, which already contains a number of eggs which he has presumably taken from other nests.*

Further upstream, BILL *steps out of the boat into some shallows. He gropes under the water and hauls up a night fishing line.* SUE *shares his disappointment when there is no catch.*

128. EXT. BUNGALOW. DAY

The dinghy pulls up at the landing stage. GRANDFATHER GEORGE, *using a stick, limps down the garden to meet them.* SUE *hands him the basket of eggs.*

GRANDFATHER GEORGE: Where's the fish? No fish, no supper. Be off with you and don't come back empty-handed.

(*He gives the boat a shove with his stick and turns back to the* house. SUE *looks weepy.* BILL *mouths some of his repertoire of swear words. From the dormer window,* DAWN *witnesses their humiliation. She laughs and waves. As* GRANDFATHER GEORGE *turns back to the house, she ducks out of sight.)*

129. EXT. WEIR. DAY
They row up to the head of the weir. BILL *casts a line and fixes the rod to the gunwale. He ties up the boat and slips over the side. He checks a net arrangement he has fixed at the base of the waterfall to snare unwary fish swimming over the weir. It is also empty.* SUE *paddles in the soft weed that grows on the steps of the weir, letting it seep between her toes.* BILL *kneels and runs his fingers through the same luminous-green weed. They become absorbed in it.* BILL *lowers his body into the water and lets himself slide over the weed.* SUE *follows suit. Soon they have discovered a glorious game, sliding like eels down the weir and plunging into the pool below. Back and forth they go. In the far distance, an air-raid siren wails. They pay no attention, so caught up are they in their pleasure.* SUE *checks the fishing line fixed to the boat. Nothing.*
SUE: I'm scared of going back without any fish. I hate Grandpa.
   (*They look up at the sound of ack-ack fire.* BILL *spots a German plane high above them.*)
BILL: Looks like a stray bomber. He's lost his squadron.
   (*Suddenly there is a blast of air and a booming explosion. Two hundred yards up river, a great plume of water spurts up. They drop flat on the steps of the weir.* BILL *peers cautiously over the rim of the waterfall.* SUE *sees his astonishment turn to a broad grin. Floating towards the weir are dozens of fish stunned by the blast. Joyously, they gather them up and throw them into the boat.*)

130. EXT. BUNGALOW. DAY
GRACE, DAWN *and the* GRANDPARENTS *all look in amazed admiration at the boat laden with fish.*
GRANDFATHER GEORGE: This is going too far, young man.
BILL: But Grandpa, you said . . .
GRANDFATHER GEORGE: I concede I was insistent, but how the devil . . .

114

(DAWN *looks sharply at the smug faces of her brother and sister.*)

DAWN: It looks a bit fishy to me.

GRACE: Could we salt them, or smoke them, do you think?

(*They fall to unloading the fish.*)

GRANDMA: It's like the feeding of the five thousand. It's a miracle.

GRANDFATHER GEORGE: Well, lad. So it's miracles now, is it?

DAWN: They'll stink the place out by morning. Why not invite all your friends to supper, Grandpa?

(*He looks up darkly from his task.*)

GRANDFATHER GEORGE: I have no friends, only relations.

131. EXT. RIVER. DAY

BILL, *now wielding the pole with great aplomb, sends the punt gliding up river.* DAWN, *heavily pregnant and languidly melancholic, lies in the cushions, a bare foot dangling in the water.* SUE *lies along the bow, trailing her arms in the river.* DAWN *stiffens as the figure of a man in uniform comes running along the riverbank. As he catches up with them, he is revealed as* BRUCE *and the uniform that of a Canadian soldier. He waves and calls to them.*

DAWN: Ignore him, the bastard.

(BILL *hesitates, but a withering look from* DAWN *keeps him on course.* BRUCE *is level with them. He calls across thirty yards of river.*)

BRUCE: Dawn! It's me!

(*She refuses even to acknowledge him. Under her breath, she instructs* BILL.)

DAWN: Keep going. Stay on this bank.

(BILL *whips up speed, keeping to the opposite side of the river from* BRUCE, *who wades out up to his knees and holds out his arms, pleadingly.*)

BRUCE: Give me a chance to explain.

(SUE *waves and smiles at him.* DAWN *glowers at her.*)

DAWN: I'm going to kill you, Sue Rohan.

(*Fully clothed, his khaki cap perched on his head,* BRUCE *swims out towards the punt. By the time he reaches the middle of the river, they are fifty yards upstream.* BRUCE *swims back to the shore. Dripping wet, he runs up the riverbank until he is well ahead of the punt and plunges in once again. This time, his course coincides with the punt. He grabs the side of the boat and hangs on, out of breath.*)

BRUCE: Couldn't write . . . Secret posting . . . came as soon as I heard about the baby.

(*DAWN grabs a paddle and forces him under the water. He pops up further down the boat.*)

I went AWOL to be with you. I'm a deserter.

(*She cracks the paddle over his head. He sinks under the water, his cap floats away. BILL rescues it. BRUCE does not reappear. They wait, become alarmed. DAWN kneels down, peers into the water.*)

DAWN: Oh, Bruce, Bruce. What have I done?

(*His head pops up inches from her face. Levering himself up on the boat, he kisses her on the mouth. She grabs his hair, smothering him with kisses.*)

I missed you so much.

(BILL *and* SUE *exchange disgusted looks.*)

132. INT. CHURCH. DAY
They are all gathered together: GRANDFATHER GEORGE,
GRANDMA, GRACE, FAITH, HOPE, CHARITY, BILL *and* SUE.
CLIVE, *in uniform, gives his daughter away.* MAC *and* MOLLY *are*
together again. All witness the quiet, subdued marriage of DAWN
and BRUCE. *The only other guests are two military policemen who*
sit at the back. They appear to be ordinary soldiers until they step
outside the church and put on their red caps.

133. EXT. CHURCH. DAY
The bridal pair come out and the VICAR, *considerably embarrassed,*
makes his excuses and backs away. A picture is taken. The Redcaps
seize BRUCE *by each arm.* DAWN *clings to him, a last kiss, and he is*
borne away. They all stand at the church doors waving to him as he
is driven away in a jeep. There is some dutiful sniffling from the
women, but since DAWN *seems quite happy, there is no need for*
sympathetic tears. GRACE *impulsively hugs* MOLLY.
GRACE: I'm so glad you could come. Here we are, all together
    again.

117

MOLLY: Happy as can be. In the old groove.
> (CLIVE *shakes* MAC's *hand warmly.*)
MAC: So you're going to be a grandfather.
CLIVE: And I'm still just a lad myself.
MAC: Don't bother to grow up. It's no fun at all.

134. EXT. BUNGALOW. DAY

The party is on the veranda. BILL *and* SUE *sit on the steps.*
GRANDFATHER GEORGE *is alone on the swing-seat.* GRACE *and
her three sisters are a string quartet. They finish a piece. The others
clap. It leaves them a little melancholy.*
GRANDFATHER GEORGE: What can you do with four
> daughters, I asked myself? A string quartet was all I could
> come up with. They hated me for making them learn.
GRACE: And now we're glad you did.
> (CLIVE *raises his glass. He is tipsy.*)
CLIVE: Here's to music. And absent friends.
MAC: And absent bridegrooms!
CLIVE: And the bride.
ALL: The bride.
CLIVE: And here's to my CO. He's wangled me a posting close
> to home. He said, 'Your house burns down, your daughter
> gets married, you're always on compassionate leave. You
> might as well stay down there!'
> (*There are cries of congratulations and encouragement.*)
GRACE: I've found a bungalow to rent up the towpath, Clive. I
> never want to leave the river again. The children have had
> such a wonderful summer.
CLIVE: Fair enough. (*Raises his glass.*) The river.
ALL: The river.
CLIVE: And loyal friends.
> (*He tips his glass at* MAC, *who squirms a little. The drink has
> made* CLIVE *sound excessively sincere and sentimental, so
> much so that if he were sober, it might seem like irony.*)
> And good and faithful wives.
> (*He points his glass at* MOLLY *and* GRACE *and waves it at the
> sisters and* DAWN.)
> We hope, and trust.

(*He laughs, and the others join in, in an awkward moment.*
GRACE *and* MOLLY *catch each other's eye.*)
And grumpy grandfathers.
(GRANDFATHER GEORGE *gets up.*)
GRANDFATHER GEORGE: Since you are shortly to join our
ranks, I throw down the gauntlet. A cricket match. You
and Mac against Bill and me. Back garden.
(*The three men and one boy rise to the challenge and file down
the side of the house to the lawn at the back.*)
CLIVE: You know Mac played for Surrey Seconds, and I opened
for the Indian Army. Are you sure . . .
(GRANDFATHER GEORGE *waves his objection aside.*)
MAC: (*To* CLIVE, *an aside*) It's an olive branch. Take it. It's the
best he can do.

135. EXT. BUNGALOW: GARDEN. DAY
GRANDFATHER GEORGE: We're putting you in to bat.
(*He hands* CLIVE *the bat, and flips the ball to* BILL *with a
broad wink.* CLIVE *takes guard against the apple tree, which is
now heavy with fruit.* BILL *bowls. The ball turns, beats the
bat.* CLIVE *pats down the grass where it bounced.*)
CLIVE: Fine delivery, Bill, good length. Turned a bit, too.
(GRANDFATHER GEORGE *hands the ball back to* BILL *and
nudges him.*)
GRANDFATHER GEORGE: (*Whispering*) Give him the you-know-
what.
BILL: Very well, Grandpa.
(BILL *delivers his googly. It bamboozles his father who pops up
a caught-and-bowled.* CLIVE *is startled. As* MAC *takes the bat,*
CLIVE *offers a warning.*)
CLIVE: I think it was a googly.
(MAC *takes guard.* BILL *bowls. He plays forward, smothering
the spin. Still no run. The next ball is pitched short.* MAC *plays
back, waits for the ball to break in from the leg which it does
more sharply than he expects. He just manages to dig it out. The
next is the googly.* MAC *does not spot it. It cuts in from the off
and clean bowls him.* GRANDFATHER GEORGE *cackles
triumphantly.*)

119

GRANDFATHER GEORGE: Googly. You didn't spot it either.
CLIVE: I taught him how and now he turns it against me.
GRANDFATHER GEORGE: The law of life. Cruel, isn't it?
MAC: The wicked old bugger.
GRANDFATHER GEORGE: This boy will make his way in the world.
> (GRANDFATHER GEORGE *slaps* BILL *on the back with such enthusiasm that he sends the boy sprawling.* CLIVE *catches him, holds him close and whispers in his ear.*)

CLIVE: I'm proud of you.
> (*Cries of alarm come from the house.* CLIVE *hears his name called. They hurry back.*)

136. INT. BUNGALOW: LIVING ROOM. DAY
The men arrive to find the women in a state of alarm. They are gathered in a knot around DAWN. BILL *pushes his way forward.*
GRACE: Clive, go for the doctor. It's Dawn. She's in labour.
> (BILL *peers between the women and catches a glimpse of* DAWN *standing arched against a chair, one hand supporting the baby's head which has appeared between her legs.*)

CLIVE: Hot water! Lots of hot water!
FAITH: What for?
CLIVE: I don't know. They always say that at the pictures.
(*He rushes out.*)

137. EXT. BUNGALOW: VERANDA. DAY
CLIVE *runs down the veranda steps.*
HOPE: She just went to the toilet, and out it came.
(MAC *joins* CLIVE *and they run to the boat and fumble
awkwardly with the oars.*)

138. INT. BUNGALOW: LIVING ROOM. DAY
GRACE *tries to be calm. She holds* DAWN *gingerly.*
GRACE: Now take deep breaths. And push.
DAWN: Why? It's coming on its own. It doesn't hurt.
(BILL *comes to* SUE's *side and they catch another glimpse of the
baby's head.* SUE *wrinkles her nose.*)
SUE: It's all sticky.
(BILL *passes clean out and crumples to the floor. Fade to
black.*)

139. EXT. GROUNDS OF A GREAT HOUSE. DAY
BILL *is running flat out, running for his life. He passes a blurred
orchard, a garden, a park.*

140. EXT. NEW BUNGALOW. DAY
BILL, *still running hard, looks over his shoulder and turns in to a
bungalow that faces on to the river.*

141. INT. NEW BUNGALOW. DAY
*The living room is cheerful and spacious. Out of the window, the sun
sets over the river.* DAWN *breast-feeds the baby, now a week or two
old.* GRACE *knits a pair of tiny leggings.* SUE *is drawing a picture.*
CLIVE *snoozes in an armchair. They are listening to Churchill on the
wireless.*
CHURCHILL (*Voice over*) . . . it is not the end. It is not the
beginning of the end. It is the end of the beginning.
(BILL *enters, flushed and panting. His eyes are bright with*

121

excitement. He goes to DAWN *and, reaching inside his shirt, pulls out a peach and hands it to her reverentially.*)

BILL: I scrumped it. I nearly got caught. They chased me for ages.

(DAWN *takes it. It looks pretty miserable. Most of the furry skin has rubbed off during its hazardous journey next to* BILL'*s skin.* DAWN'*s first impulse is to make a sarcastic comment, but in her new maturity, she bites it back and smiles.*)

DAWN: You did that for me, and on the last day of your holidays?

(BILL *blushes.*)

BILL: Well, for the baby, really.

DAWN: Thank you, Billy, from the baby and me.

142. INT. GRANDFATHER GEORGE'S CAR. DAY

GRANDFATHER GEORGE *drives his old Armstrong Siddeley Sapphire along the river towpath. Beside him sits a very morose* BILL *wearing a school cap, with satchel, gasmask, and a suitcase on his lap.* GRANDFATHER GEORGE *adjusts the advance/retard lever and glares at the sullen boy.*

GRANDFATHER GEORGE: You miserable little tripe-hound. I'm the one who should be fed up, sacrificing my last sup of black-market petrol to take you to school.

BILL: I have to live in Rosehill Avenue as well.

GRANDFATHER GEORGE: Only till they get you into the local school.

BILL: With Mrs Evans. I hate her.

GRANDFATHER GEORGE: You'll be home for the week-ends. Now shut up, or walk.

(*They pass a film unit setting up equipment on the river bank. Extras dressed as soldiers – German, British, American – lounge, smoke and drink tea.*)

Strapping fellows playing silly buggers with a war on. Outrageous.

(BILL *cranes back watching as long as he can.*)

143. EXT. SCHOOL. DAY

The car draws up outside the school entrance. A grim wall surrounds the institution and BILL *gets out, head hung low, and walks towards the gate as though to the gallows.* GRANDFATHER GEORGE *watches from the car. He grips the steering wheel angrily. A teacher strides past.* GRANDFATHER GEORGE *shouts after him out of the window.*

GRANDFATHER GEORGE: All you do is knock the sense out of them and fill them up with muck.

144. EXT. SCHOOLYARD. DAY
As BILL *enters, he is astonished to see hundreds of children in a state of delirious celebration. Boys fling their caps in the air. They cheer. They whoop. They run amok. Behind them lie the smouldering ruins of the school.* BILL *cheers louder than anyone. He remembers his grandfather, turns on his heel and runs back to the road.*

145. EXT. SCHOOL. DAY
GRANDFATHER GEORGE *is awkwardly turning the car in the road.
He drives off.* BILL *runs flat out and comes up to the window,
shouting.*

BILL: Grandpa! There's no school! It's been hit by a bomb!
    (GRANDFATHER GEORGE *slows up.*)
GRANDFATHER GEORGE: I have to hand it to you, Bill, you
    come up with some good ones. Go back and take your
    medicine.
    (*He drives off leaving* BILL *stranded. A fire engine and ARP
    vehicles race up to the school. They pass* GRANDFATHER
    GEORGE *and doubt shows in his face. He stops, gets out. Boys
    are spilling out of the school, cheering.* BILL *runs up to him.*)
BILL: It's true.
GRANDFATHER GEORGE: You're much more convincing when
    you're making it up.
    (*They get into the car.*)
BILL: Grandpa, if you think of something hard enough, can you
    make it happen?
GRANDFATHER GEORGE: Apparently so.
    (*A barking laugh wells up and escapes his control. It bursts
    forth in great waves like a flood that has been dammed up for
    years.*)

146. EXT. RIVER: DAY
GRANDFATHER GEORGE'*s laugh, and* BILL'*s too, ring out over
the autumn river which beckons to* BILL *with the promise of stolen
days.*

A day at the seaside (1933). *Left to right:* Me, my mother, Wendy, my father.

A day at the seaside. *Left to right:* Sarah Miles (Grace), Geraldine Muir (Sue), David Hayman (Clive), Susan Wooldridge (Molly), Sebastian Rice Edwards (Bill), Derek O'Connor (Mac), Sarah Langton (as the young Dawn).

On the reverse of this photo is inscribed: *L. cpl G. Boorman, 5th East Surrey Regt, Sailed for India Oct 29 1914.* He later transferred to the Indian Army.

Playing my father (Clive), David Hayman.

Postscript

My sister Wendy (Dawn) took her baby to Canada at the end of
the war. She had another child, a girl. Wendy sent welcome
food parcels in the grim years of shortage after the war. She
came home to visit in 1950 and decided not to return. It was the
end of her marriage. She and her husband were wed as children. They grew up in different ways. For the past twenty years
she has been happily married to a Cornish boatbuilder and
fisherman. They live in Mevagissey. She was just sixteen when
her son Robert was born. I was eight, so Robert is only eight
years younger than me. He was like a brother to me and she was
more like a sister to him than a mother. He went to art school. I
have told how he inherited Grandpa's clarinet laugh and his difficulty in taking life seriously. Perhaps Robert got his inven-
tiveness from Grandpa too. When he was still at college he
helped Wendy's husband to build a house. He then sat down
and devised ways of doing it more quickly, better and more
cheaply. By the time he was twenty-five he was a millionaire
and owned a large factory in Truro in which he made system-
built houses. They were assembled on site in just three days.
Soon he was putting up twenty or thirty a week. He had to buy
land to put the houses on. There was some two years' lead time
to develop the land and gain all the necessary permissions, so he
needed to acquire a huge land bank. Then came the oil crisis of
1973. Development land fell in value by 50 per cent. Since
Robert borrowed two-thirds of the money to acquire the land,
the banks foreclosed. He had no outlet for the houses, and was
forced to stop production at his factory. Two hundred and fifty
men were put out of work. Robert had ploughed all his profits
back into the business. He was bankrupt and penniless.

He had a good laugh over that. He was fed up with building
houses, delighted to start afresh. All he salvaged was some
antique furniture and his collection of modern paintings. He

131

packed them up and set sail for America where he sold what he had for enough to get a new start. He now lives in Los Angeles with his wife and three children. I see him when I go over and we always have a good laugh together.

My sister Angela (Sue) has two grown-up daughters and lives in Rottingdean by the sea close to our father's beloved Brighton, but she hankers for the river and is searching for a Thames-side bungalow.

Bruce eventually married again, to a delightful woman, and they live in Ontario, having moved from his native Montreal. He has recently retired.

The film studios at Shepperton were built by Alexander Korda and just after the war they were in full spate of production. They often shot location scenes by the river and I remember watching and thinking what a good idea it was to rearrange the world so that things came out the way you wanted them or imagined they could be.

My best friend and I tried for jobs as clapper boys. He succeeded; I did not. I tried to write. The *Manchester Guardian* published some of my essays. At eighteen I was chairman of a weekly BBC radio programme about the arts for young people. I went to all the film studios and recorded interviews with directors and technicians. After National Service in the Army I finally got a job in the cutting rooms as a trainee assistant editor.

My father came out of the Army in 1945, thoroughly disillusioned. Far from escaping his pen-pushing job, he had pushed a pen and tapped a typewriter in the RASC. What a comedown from sticking pigs in India.

Mac became crippled with arthritis and my mother tended him. Mac's wife and my father both suffered pangs of jealousy, but Mac was in constant pain and my mother refused to abandon him. Her presence was the only amelioration for his suffering. He was dying. She sat with him, radiant with love, no longer troubling to conceal it from the world. My father brooded in the shadows, while my mother's light fell upon his dying friend. She was in a state of grace, and that grace embraced Mac, and Grace I named her in this story.

132

My mother, Ivy Chapman (Grace).

How the film was made,
and nearly wasn't

I completed the first draft script at my home in Ireland during the two-week doldrums that followed Christmas 1985. Given its nature, I was not at all sanguine about getting financial backing. I showed it to Jake Eberts who liked it very much, but predicted it would be a 'tough sell'. I have a development deal with Jake's company, Allied Filmmakers. Although I did not ask him to put up money for the script, he agreed to pay for the preparation of a budget and some initial design work, which was necessary to get the information to *make* a budget. I sent it to my agent, Jeff Berg, at ICM in Los Angeles. His response was extremely enthusiastic and he pledged himself to getting a deal made.

Our first budget came in at around 10 million dollars to the shock and horror of some studio assessors who got the impression of a rather small intimate picture. I had never seen it thus, nor intended it so.

The strategy Jake and I planned was to get a good advance on video sales in the US and have Goldcrest market the picture in all other territories so that the North American distributors would be asked for only a modest sum.

Our aim was something like this:

Foreign sales (Goldcrest)	$3 million
US Video	$3 million
US Theatrical distribution	$4 million

The script was liked and admired by many of the major studios, but it was considered commercially dubious. Fox came very close, but finally backed away. Warners felt it conflicted with *Empire of the Sun*, a Spielberg project about a small boy during the fall of Singapore. One by one the 'passes' came in: Universal, MGM, UA, Tri-Star, Orion, Paramount.

Meanwhile Fred Turner, Managing Director of Rank, expressed effusive enthusiasm for the script and Jake began to negotiate. Fred said he would be interested not just for the UK, but might put up 3 million dollars for the whole of 'foreign'. Unfortunately, he was unable to persuade his board, who turned it down flat.

The first glimmer of hope came from France. Paul Rassam, head of AMLF Distributors in Paris, had had a huge success with *The Emerald Forest* and without a moment's hesitation pledged 500,000 American dollars. This was very important for us. Paul's judgement is greatly respected and many distributors around the world follow his lead.

Bill (Sebastian Rice Edwards) and Sue (Geraldine Muir) fishing on the weir at Shepperton where John Boorman, and his mother before him, played as children.

John Boorman directs Sebastian Rice Edwards for the scene
on the weir.

Camera Platform constructed on the weir, with frogmen ready
in case of any mishaps.

139

Design drawing by Tony Pratt of the Gang's den in a
bombed building.

We approached Simon Relph at British Screen. He liked the
project, but after examining the budget felt he could not support it unless it was 'costed down' to the level of a 'British' picture as against an 'International' one. He spent some time with
Michael Dryhurst, my co-producer, and me and was very helpful. Following his advice we cut salaries by 20 per cent across
the board, knowing that it would mean losing some technicians
we wanted and taking lesser ones – which in fact happened.
This was particularly painful where Michael Dryhurst and
Tony Pratt, the designer, were concerned since I had already
agreed their deals. Tony's agent advised him against accepting
a reduced salary, but Tony very much wanted to do the picture.
Hope and Glory is our fourth collaboration. He eventually took
the lower fee. I shall make it up to them out of the profits, if
there are any. On this basis Simon Relph pledged his support.

The scene from the film. The set was built in Bray Studios.

The maximum he was allowed to invest in any one film was £700,000, but he felt half a million was the most he could offer us, if his board approved, and if we could agree terms on which he would recover his investment.

Jake's next target was Channel 4. They had achieved one of their best audience figures when they showed *Excalibur* and I had produced one of their first successes in the *Film on Four* series, Neil Jordan's *Angel*. Jeremy Isaacs's policy has rescued and revived British films. His judicious backing had made possible films like Tarkovsky's *The Sacrifice, Paris, Texas, My Beautiful Laundrette, Room with a View*. Calling in my credit and his own, Jake pleaded our case and prised out a promise of £350,000. Unfortunately, the money would not be paid over until they were able to show the film, two years after its cinema release. Nevertheless we could enter it in the ledger.

Jake's major play had to be the United States market, which

141

if video, TV and cable is included represents 70 per cent of the world income of an English-language movie. He went to André Blay, Head of Embassy Home Entertainment. They had made considerable profits on the video sale of *The Emerald Forest*, of which, because of an unfortunate deal, we received no part. Jake was not slow to suggest to André that he had a moral debt to pay. Blay expressed interest and talked of a million-dollar advance, escalating to match the prints and advertising budget of a US distributor up to a maximum of 3.5 million dollars. The trouble was we had no distributor so all we could rely on was 1 million dollars out of the US.

While Jake was battling away in Los Angeles a new possibility arose in London. Golan and Globus, owners of the Cannon Group, had bought EMI. The acquisition was greeted with suspicion, anger and chauvinism, as with it, the only major film-making and exhibition force fell out of British control. When Cannon announced it would make thirty films a year, most of the barking dogs rolled on to their backs or at least wagged their tails.

I phoned Menahem Golan and told him I had a project.

'Come and talk to me,' he said.

'When?'

'When you like.'

'I'll be there in an hour.'

It was only their second day in charge. The switchboard receptionist had not yet worked out the difference between Menahem Golan and Yoram Globus.

'Both names sound the same to me,' she complained. I gave her some helpful advice.

'Globus is the plump one; Golan the fat one.'

As I was shown in Menahem was conducting at least four meetings simultaneously. Supplicants were hunched or cramped in every corner and crevice. EMI employees with stunned expressions wandered past – fired, or rehired or transferred. Michael Winner sat at Menahem's elbow offering witty and scabrous interpretations of the local natives' behaviour. I looked out of the window and there was Producer Jeremy Thomas standing across the street looking up at us with a wry expression, wondering, I expect, if Cannon would honour the deal he had forged with EMI.

I made several attempts to tell my story, but each one was frustrated by the intervention of burning issues requiring the great man's judgement. I apologetically mentioned the parochial Englishness of the piece. Suddenly I found myself with his full attention. The very thing that put off all the others made it attractive to Menahem. It was the perfect project to confound those critics who were predicting Cannon would make only crass multi-national movies. What better subject to proclaim his commitment to British films!

'Listen,' he said, 'I don't have time to read it, but if you like it, I like it. You don't want to make a flop, nor do I. How much?'

'Nine point five,' I said. (Simon Relph had singed half a million from the margins.)

'Do it for seven and a half and we have a deal.'

I winced and shook my head. He took that as an affront to his integrity.

'I'll tell you how we work. Directors love us. You become one of the family. Yoram and I will be the producers. We give you everything you want as long as it's not more than seven.'

I had just lost half a million dollars. I must have looked glum. He tried to convince me. He reached for the phone.

'Zeffirelli will tell you. He never wants to work for another producer, only us. Franco will tell you.' He started to dial, but Globus rushed in, waving a sheaf of papers.

'Worse. Much worse. Their books smell. These are not good men, Menahem.' He wafted the papers at Golan, who sniffed them.

'Forget it,' he said. 'We just made a deal for John Boorman's picture.' He turned to me. 'What's it called again? He's going to make it for seven – maximum.' He looked me in the eye. 'We've got to get it under seven.' My time was up. He led me to the door.

'We're leaving in the morning. Talk to Otto Plaschkes. He's going to look after creative matters for us in London.'

They announced their intention of making *Hope and Glory* in

German Pilot (Charley Boorman) drops from a 120-ft crane.

Cannes, along with thirty other projects.

I wrote a new draft of the script eliminating two expensive set-piece scenes, reduced the amount of night work, and effecting other economies. In this way, and by deferring my fees as writer, director and producer, we managed to squeeze the budget down to 7.5 million dollars, although Michael Dryhurst and I both felt uneasy about being able to hold to this figure.

I duly reported this to Otto who had read and loved the script. He sent his recommendation to Menahem in Los Angeles, who promptly telexed his reply: 'We'll go ahead if you can make it for 5 million dollars.'

Meanwhile Jake was making better progress with André Blay at Embassy. I was summoned to Cannes. I proceeded to the

Hôtel du Cap where Blay and his lieutenants were living in pampered purdah from the vulgar Festival down the coast. André has an air about him of decency, of detached amusement and quiet intelligence. Jake arrived looking his most wolfish. André and his men were slightly offguard, taking it easy after the rigours of the management buyout they had just negotiated with Coca Cola, the owners of the company. Jake proposed that Embassy should put up the whole budget and he demonstrated how foreign sales and a US distribution deal would pay off most of their investment leaving them with the video rights at a bargain price, plus the lion's share of profits points in the picture.

Jake juggled the figures, making lightning calculations in his head. André would not commit, but came very close. He was hovering, wavering, tempted. After all, the video rights of most important films are tied to a major distributor. The independent video distributor must invest in films up front to ensure a flow of product. He was clearly enchanted with Jake's acrobatic arithmetic. Finally, he agreed to come to London after Cannes and take a look at our designs and plans.

He duly arrived at Twickenham Studios, saw our layouts, listened to my predictions about what the film would be and, still harbouring reservations about its commercial prospects, he pledged his troth. There was one reservation: he was obliged to seek the approval of Coca Cola. However, since the company would be his in a couple of weeks this was a formality that could be overlooked. He agreed to fund the pre-production right away. It was just in the nick of time. It was mid-May. Since there were so many children in the movie, it was essential to shoot during the school holidays. We also needed summer for the river scenes. Construction of the sets had to begin right away if we were to start in late July. Had André hesitated or procrastinated another couple of weeks, I would have been obliged to delay the film until the following year. A movie gathers a certain momentum, which, if checked, is hard to achieve again.

We had already made the momentous decision to build Rosehill Avenue, the street of semis in which I was born. When Michael Dryhurst gave the go-ahead to Syd Nightingale, our

The street under construction.

Bill (Sebastian Rice Edwards) and Sue (Geraldine Muir) in the
bomb-damaged street set. Barrage balloons and the London sky-line
are achieved through tricks of perspective.

construction manager, an army of men descended on the deserted airfield at Wisley where we proposed to build it. André
Blay had baulked at the cost of this massive construction.
Surely, he protested, we could find a street of thirties semis
where we could shoot the picture. We had looked. Existing
streets were bristling with TV aerials, the kerbs jammed with
cars, and festooned with modern accretions like double glazing
and metal garage doors. Even then, the occupants might not
have taken kindly to their houses being bombed and burned.
The only hope was a street that was abandoned, about to be de-
molished to make way for a motorway, but no such situation
occurred, nor would it have quite worked if it had.

Building the street allowed us to express its raw newness, its
treelessness, an absolute monotony. It would be one of the two
central metaphors of the movie. The Street. The River.

147

Tony Pratt contrived a triumphant concept. On each side of the road we built the façades of six pairs of semis on a framework of scaffolding. At one end a cut-out was placed across the street and painted with houses that appeared to recede into perspective, giving a child's remembrance of a street that reached into infinity. In the far, far distance were further cut-outs of the skyline of London including a movable St Paul's Cathedral, which could be shunted from one side to the other to suit the angle of each particular shot. The other end of the street was a crescent with a cut-out of a gasometer. The Rohan house was actually built of brick and wood since it had to be burned, which of course would reveal what lay underneath the façade. A range of back gardens extended on one side, leading to allotments and an abandoned building site. We used the backs of the houses on the other side as a backdrop for an area of bombed ruins. All in all, the multiple set covered more than fifty acres, probably the largest set built in Britain since the war.

Four weeks into construction Jake called with shocking news. Coca Cola had decided not to sell Embassy Home Entertainment to André Blay after all, and had castigated him for entering into my deal without their approval. He sued Coke; Coke sued him. There was deadlock. Embassy ground to a standstill and our weekly cash flow abruptly stopped. There was insufficient money to cover the wage bill at the end of the week. Jake stepped forward with a cheque from Allied to tide us over, and Michael Dryhurst dashed down to Wisley and gave two weeks' notice to the men.

In Los Angeles, my agent, Jeff Berg, and the redoubtable Edgar Gross who handles my business affairs laid siege to Embassy and Coca Cola. Two weeks later, just as the notices were expiring, the matter had still not been settled although Jeff had persuaded the Coca Cola director Frank Biondi that they had a moral obligation to fund us.

We calculated that I would have to find out of my own pocket some £35,000 in winding-up costs to cancel the picture; Jake would lose his £65,000 advance too.

At 11 p.m. on Thursday night, Jeff called to say that Coca

Cola would resume payments. At eight o'clock the next morning, we were going to close down the picture.

Coca Cola subsequently sold Embassy to another group and part of that deal was that Columbia (which Coke also owned) would undertake to distribute the film theatrically in the States. At the very last gasp, the movie was saved. We re-engaged the men and started up again. There was a loss of momentum. Suspicion and uncertainty were hard to dispel and some men deserted. Hearing of our troubles the various unions insisted that we deposit substantial bonds with them as a condition of continuing. All in all, it put us back a week or more and cost us around £60,000.

David Puttnam's appointment as the new chief of Columbia Pictures brought a fresh confidence and stability. He gave *Hope and Glory* his full backing and stepped up his investment to take the UK rights as well as the US. This took British Screen off the hook and allowed Simon Relph to use that money elsewhere. So, as it turned out, this most English of subjects was being financed by some twenty distributors around the world with the only British money being Channel 4's TV buy, which would not be paid for some three years.

We commenced photography on 4 August 1986, shot for fifty-five days, with the final wrap on 21 October. Post-production was completed on 14 February 1987.